Love Will Find a Way

ANJI NOLAN

author of *The Cormorant Club* and *Desperate Obsession*

CRIMSON ROMANCE

F+W Media, Inc.

This edition published by
Crimson Romance
an imprint of F+W Media, Inc.
10151 Carver Road, Suite 200
Blue Ash, Ohio 45242
www.crimsonromance.com

ISBN 10: 1-4405-6785-9
ISBN 13: 978-1-4405-6785-8
eISBN 10: 1-4405-6786-7
eISBN 13: 978-1-4405-6786-5

For Dad, who gave me wings,
For Mum, who let me fly,
And for Booj, who was always there to pick up the pieces.
xoxo

Acknowledgments

Thank you Jennifer Lawler and the stellar team at Crimson Romance for your encouragement and support. Thanks to Susan Permenter, and Karl Gazzolo Sr., for your input after wading through early drafts. And to Sandi and T.W. Bodiford for introducing me to fried catfish, and the capabilities of the V-tail Bonanza. And to my muse, Captain Bron Ama, sincere thanks for your friendship and aviation expertise.

Chapter One

The rhythmic beating of wings alerted her, and Emily looked up to see a gull hovering fifteen feet or so above the chaise on which she reclined.

"It's a thief you know," said an accent-tinged voice.

Startled, she turned. "Who's a thief?" She shielded her eyes against the sun, and recognized the elegantly dressed blond from the night before. "Oh hi, Jack Clemmons, isn't it?"

He took off his sunglasses, revealing ice blue eyes. "You remembered."

"How could anyone forget you after such generous contributions to the awards dinner?"

"I'd rather you remembered my sparkling wit and personality."

Emily smiled. "It was a receiving line. I don't recall any chit-chat."

"Yet I remembered the tall redhead with green eyes."

"Occupational hazard, there aren't many of us left." Emily swung her legs from the chaise and retied her pareo about her hips. "So, Jack, I'm guessing the accent is South African."

"You would be correct, and you are American."

She giggled. "No shit, Sherlock, what gave me away?"

"You're very blunt, aren't you?"

"Is that a problem?"

Jack slipped his glasses back on as Emily dug hers from her bag. "Not at all; I like a strong woman. Did you have fun last night?"

"I'd have had more if I'd won the diamond tennis bracelet."

He held out a solid practical hand. "So, come take a look at the bird." Jack helped Emily to her feet, and led her to the parapet. "See the hotel's seafood delivery."

"And?"

He pointed. "Look up there."

The gull had left the terrace and perched on a flagpole across the street. With wings outstretched, it bounced wildly and squawked in agitation as a deliveryman hoisted a basket of seafood on his shoulder.

"Now watch the cheeky moocher," Jack said.

As soon as the fishmonger disappeared down the alley, the gull launched off the pole, and swooped onto the cart. There, head cocked and wings extended, it plucked an expensive tidbit from its kelpy resting-place. It rose high again, and overhead the terrace, dropped its cargo. A large snail hit the ground, bounced twice, and came to rest against the parapet. The bird swooped down beside the mollusk, and tentatively poked the cracked shell to see if its beak would penetrate. When it would not, the hungry flyer danced around the stricken escargot, webbed-feet slapping aggressively on concrete.

Coming from the city, Emily had never seen anything like the seagull dance, and as she watched in rapt fascination the bird regrouped, took the snail back in its beak, and for a second time, rose in the air letting the mollusk plummet to the unforgiving terrace below. This time, a large chunk of shell broke off, exposing the delicacy inside, and before another could swoop in and steal its hard-earned meal, the gull plucked out the spongy gastropod, swallowed it down, and returned to its purloining perch across the street.

"Crafty little critter, isn't it?" said Jack.

"Might say the same about you; how long were you standing behind me?"

"A couple of minutes. I didn't mean to disturb your sunbathing, but I couldn't resist letting you know why the dinner I'm about to buy you is so expensive."

"What makes you think I'm going to dinner with you?" She returned to the chaise.

"Because you said you would."

"Excuse me?"

"I clearly made an impression the last time we spoke."

"And when exactly was that?"

"You don't remember Walvis Bay Holdings's diamond shipment? Last week; you expedited the gems transfer to the clearing house after the courier screwed up. My father, in his usual accusatory fashion, thought the gems had been stolen, and you said you'd make it your mission to locate them before leaving for Monaco."

"That was you? You sound different."

"Last week I was calling ship-to-shore."

"You called me at JFK airport from a boat?"

"My father wanted his gems in-house before he left the U.S. A business colleague said call Emiline Wilks at Transcontinental, she'll make it happen. So I did."

"Your father called Europe from the U.S. to have you check on a shipment clearing in New York?"

"Yup, he called me here, to call you there, to do that."

"Holy Christmas, that's one convoluted chain of command."

"Par for my father's course. He refuses to get personally involved with us peasants. Gets just about anybody, to do anything, at any time he wants."

"You know the chance of anyone stealing a shipment from Transcontinental is pretty remote. Only a couple of us know how to access the vault, and the courier guards have the pickups timed to the minute."

"Doesn't wash with my father; he sees the bad in everybody."

"Now there's a boatload of familial resentment."

"You better believe it. He has me on a leash so tight, I about choke myself. So, are we on for dinner or not?"

"I'm not sure. My roommate is due in today. Besides, Transcontinental really frowns on employees accepting gratuities."

"Female roommate?"

"Something like that."

"Well that clarifies things."

"She's a lesbian."

"And you are…"

Emily smiled. "Not."

"Boyfriend with you?"

"I'm a little old for 'boyfriends'."

"You know what I mean."

"There is someone, back in the states. Is that going to prevent you from taking me to dinner?"

"Don't see him with you, so probably not."

"Then we'll say no more about him and move on."

"Good. And my offer is not a gratuity." Jack pulled up a chair. "Look around. It appears we're the only people under sixty staying at this hotel, and since we're both going to get hungry at some point, why not eat together. It'll be fun, and we can talk about something other than stock portfolios, how much we dropped on the tables last night, or who died when, from what, and left whom, God knows how much money."

"You're staying here, too?"

"No. At the moment I'm a glorified tour guide living on *The Adamas*—that's my father's yacht."

"How exotic." Emily extended her hand. "But a promise is a promise. Hello Jack, my friends call me Emily."

"Well I'm pleased you so generously brought me into the realm of 'friend' and might I suggest dinner at six. Shall I meet you in the lobby or come to your room?"

"Umm, let me think about that…" Emily tapped a finger on the arm of the chaise.

"Oh come on now, you didn't think I was suggesting—"

"Suggesting what, Mr. Clemmons?"

Jack blushed. "Er, nothing. I'll be in the lobby at six." He smiled thinly and walked away.

• • •

Emily saw Jack as the elevator doors opened. And not knowing where they would be going, but realizing most anywhere in Monte Carlo was dressy, she had opted to wear a silk faille two-piece, with Manolos and matching purse.

Jack walked forward and kissed her routinely on both cheeks. "A vision in pale blue. How lovely, Misook, I believe."

"How perceptive. Are you a buyer for Saks in your spare time?"

He smiled. "And the shoes?"

"Don't tell me you know they're Manolo Blahniks?"

"I was going to say, can you walk in them?'"

"What did you have in mind? If you're thinking the Appalachian Trail we could have a problem; but if it's just a turn around the square, I'm your gal."

"Then, Ms. Emily Sarcasm, you are indeed my gal." He proffered his arm. "Walk this way."

She linked his arm as he led her under the cavernous dome of The Hermitage's *Jardin d'Hiver*, and as they stepped out into Monaco's balmy evening air, he paused. "Roommate arrive?"

"Yes, finally. I was in the shower and didn't even see her. She stopped at the room long enough to ditch her bag, and then went to the casino. She drives me nuts with her gambling. She's always working on 'her system' or looking for a cockamamie angle to make money. I'm sick of bailing her out and listening to her sob stories."

"Sob stories?" asked Jack.

"The tables are rigged. Somebody stole my stash. A compulsive gambler's usual excuses."

"Look up there." Jack pointed to a street corner lamppost.

"What are they?"

"Cameras. They are everywhere. The Monaco Tourist Authority brags that you could leave a million bucks in a convertible and if it was stolen, they'd have the thief before he got to the border."

"Well, that takes care of that excuse. What about the rigged tables?"

"Now that's out of my sphere of knowledge; I never gamble. What little money my father pays me is precious."

"Maybe you should meet her and try and impart that wisdom; I'm getting nowhere. In fact, some things have happened lately to make me realize it's time we parted ways. Anyway, I sent her a message at the casino saying I was having dinner with you. And I'm sort of glad I wasn't around when she arrived. Her mood, which is not good at the best of times, will not have improved by sitting in the Geneva airport for twenty-four hours waiting to use her staff pass."

"Isn't getting all psyched up for a trip and being left hanging irritating?"

"For those of us who aren't rich enough to live on a yacht in Monte Carlo harbor, getting a free pass or paying ten percent is worth the hassle."

"Direct, but point taken. Keep walking, Ms. Emily, I can see we're going to get along like a house on fire."

Along with Jack and Emily, many others had chosen to promenade before the impressive Belle Époque buildings of the Square Beaumarchais, and as the smell of coffee and expensive perfume permeated the air, Emily enjoyed the solid feel of Jack's arm, and the way his body fit next to hers.

"So, Jack, what if I'd been a frumpy matron, with bleached blonde hair and ill-fitting dentures. Would we still be going out to dinner?"

"You think I'm that shallow?"

"Just saying."

They stopped at Raffi's, an open air café bustling with patrons. "So, here we are," said Jack, leading her to a table replete with canapés and an open bottle of champagne.

"I see you called ahead," said Emily.

"It pays to be prepared." Jack poured the wine. "Being airline staff, you obviously get to travel anywhere. Have you been here before?"

"First time. This champagne is yummy, and I love canapés. I could happily make a meal of them. How about you?"

"Canapés?"

She giggled. "Monaco; you live here all the time?"

"No, my father has me organize tours for his business associates. This is just one venue for me. I stay on the yacht until it loads up, then I decamp to The Hermitage."

"So that's why you were loitering about."

"I'm not sure The Hermitage would approve of anyone loitering about."

"It is a bit old school,' said Emily. "But I really do like it. I sat in the lobby for hours yesterday imagining all the famous people who'd checked in."

"You know it's stood on the Square Beaumarchais since the early 1900s, and while most people know about Monte Carlo's casino because it has been in several movies, I think The Hermitage is the more beautiful building. Did you know it's a registered historical monument?"

Emily giggled. "That your tour-guide speech?"

"Yup, that's the opening salvo."

"Sounds good."

"I hate it. Standing around, spouting a load of nonsense to people who don't give a rat's ass. It's demoralizing." Jack took a large swallow of champagne. "I'd give my right arm to chuck it all in."

"You work for your father. Tell him you're not happy and want to do something else."

"Wish I could. It's not that simple."

"Why? I'm presuming you're over twenty-one."

"I got into a bit of trouble back home. I'm under court orders."

"What did you do, murder someone?"

"Not quite."

"Uh oh. How 'not quite'?"

"Motor vehicle fatality. Some friends and I got a little drunk—"

"A little?"

"Okay, a lot. You really want to know? My story isn't pretty."

"Stuff that makes anyone as bent out of shape as you appear to be, rarely is. I'm a big girl; let's hear it."

"The trouble started at my graduation ceremony."

"In South Africa?"

Jack nodded. "Cape Town University, I studied international finance. I was valedictorian and me a bunch of friends started celebrating that—and our freedom from school—hours before the speeches ended."

"Okay, we got the drunk driver admission. What next?"

"After polishing off two magnums of champagne, a bottle of vodka and a fifth of gin, we piled into three convertibles and headed for the beach."

"And is that where the bad stuff happened?"

Jack frowned. "You gonna let me get through this or what?"

"Sorry; airline worker, deadlines are a religion."

"With the booze gone, someone suggested we hit The Palms. It's a ritzy beach resort on the dunes, but they refused us entry, 'cos we were all so cooked. And I said 'let's try Nelly Palmers'. It was a ways off, but they'd serve a pickled warthog, if it had a cent. I was the only one who knew the way, so I took the lead."

"When you knew you were too looped to drive?"

"I'm not proud of that," answered Jack. "But we wanted some fun. Needed to let off steam and celebrate our freedom. I admit I was driving fast. But the roads were empty, and everyone seemed okay with it. Nobody said slow down so I hurtled on. Then as I rounded a corner, I misjudged the curve, and ended up fishtailing for half a mile."

"Did you crash?"

"No. But the wall of dust I kicked up wiped out visibility for the guys behind me. I was totally unaware anything had happened until there was an explosion."

"Jesus!"

"Pretty much my thought." Jack took another sip of wine. "As I looked in my rearview, a huge orange fireball was where my friends should be. I slammed my car into reverse and my friend Rick and I jumped out, and the girls with us took off to get help.

"At first, we just stood and watched as pieces of metal shot from the mushroom cloud rising into the sky. We were helpless. Jimbo, driver of the second car, had veered across the road and hit a power pole, which snapped in two. The front of his car was folded round the stake like a giant fortune cookie, and the overhead wires had snapped, catapulting the top of the pole across the road."

"Oh my God," said Emily, hand to her mouth.

"It sliced through the third car, like a cheese cutter." Jack paused to collect himself. "Then I heard a scream. Rick said it was my imagination, but it wasn't. I couldn't see much through the smoke, but I had to do something and stumbled forward. A wall of flame exploded out of nowhere and when I hit the ground, I felt a body. I pulled it from the flames, and Rick who was pre-med, stayed with them as I began to circle the area looking for other survivors. There was another explosion. I recall being launched upward. Then everything went black."

"Jack, I am so sorry. I assume your friends died."

His eyes glazed and he nodded. "Everything was my fault."

"You tried to help; there was nothing you could do."

"Seven of my closest friends died because of my reckless stupidity."

Emily touched his arm. "It was an accident, Jack, one of those awful inexplicable things that just happen."

"Apparently the judge trying my case wasn't entirely of the same opinion. If it hadn't been for my father's influence I'd be in jail now."

"So that's a good thing."

"No, it isn't. Before we left the court, my father not only convinced the judge that to prevent another drunken episode he should retain control over me until I was thirty, but also that I was unfit to handle the responsibility of an inheritance left me by my mother."

"That's not all bad. How old are you now?"

"I'll be twenty-nine in a few weeks."

"So another year or so and you're free."

"It's not that easy."

"I smell a cop-out, Mr. Clemmons. Are we feeling just a tad sorry for our-self?"

Jack smiled indulgently. "I told you, my major at university was international finance. You can't disappear for years and pick up where you left off. Things move so fast, you have to be right on top of trends or you're lost."

"Your life isn't so bad," Emily replied. "You live on a yacht, travel the world—"

"A penniless lackey at my father's beck and call."

"We're all at somebody's beck and call. You just have to make the best of the hand you're dealt."

"Oh, my, Miss Emiline Wilks, where were you three years ago?"

"Let's see; Fiji, meeting Bill."

"Are you going to tell me about him?"

"He was opening a resort and we hit it off after I helped him with something."

Jack smiled. "Much like you helped me."

"Yeah, that's me, the all-American Girl Scout."

Jack took Emily's hand. "I have badges you can earn."

"I'm sure you do, but here's our waiter, so just tell him what you'd like to eat."

Jack grinned and kissed her knuckles.

•••

During dinner, Emily was amazed how much Jack knew about the world, but how unaware he was of the effect his good looks and attentive demeanor had on a woman. The two conversed in bits and pieces of languages they'd learned on their travels, swapped horror stories about lost luggage, and laughed uncontrollably about misadventures with foreign plumbing. They criticized everything about monopolistic communication companies, and the lack of a universal electrical system. And when it appeared a crowd was gathering, and their table was needed, Emily suggested they return to The Hermitage for a nightcap.

Emily led Jack to a quiet spot in The Hermitage's lounge, and a waiter immediately attended them. "Coffee all right, or do you want something stronger?" she asked.

"Coffee's good. I do love how civilized this place is. They really don't mind if you sit all night and just watch the world go by. Now, tell me about the boyfrie—sorry, *gentleman* friend back in America. I assume you argued and are now unattached."

"And you would be wrong. I'm not only here for the awards dinner. I'm working out an issue."

"Oh?"

"Bill and I have the same philosophies, we like many of the same things. But when it comes right down to it, his age gives him limitations. He's a lot older than me; twenty-six years, in fact."

Jack whistled.

"Thank you for that unnecessary musical interlude."

Jack grinned. "Sorry, the age thing was a bit of a shock. Please go on."

"Bill is extremely special. He helped me when I needed a friend. He's supportive, and generous. He has the wherewithal to give me most everything I want—"

"I hear you. That 'most anything' will put a spanner in the works every time."

"You've got some pretty sarcastic notions for a grown man who appears to be completely controlled by his father. What are you, twenty-nine going on twelve?"

"Touché, Ms. Emily, I now have official warning that you bite."

"Sorry, but I've known Bill three years, and he's pretty much everything to me."

"But you're still single, so I assume he's married."

"There you go again. No, he's not."

"Then what's holding him back?"

"He wants marriage, but I'm still thinking about it."

"After three years. Why?"

"Because it's none of your beeswax, that's why."

Jack ran a finger across an eyebrow. "Now I'm sorry. We were getting on so well, I thought we could be honest."

"You're right. If our relationship is so perfect, why am I having dinner and flirting with a virtual stranger? I can only say it's complicated."

"I'm quite good at complicated. Tell me; my shoulder is at your disposal."

"I want kids," said Emily sadly. "Lots of them. But Bill caught mumps at the wrong time and he's sterile."

"Now that's a biggie. Couldn't you adopt?"

"He says he's too old."

"Then I see your dilemma."

"Do you want kids?"

Jack raised an eyebrow. "Is that an invitation?"

"Be serious."

Jack covered her hand with his. "I am. I'm very attracted to you; can't you feel it?"

"You just met me. You have no idea who I am."

"Don't care. We feel right, that's good enough for me."

"Well, Mr. Clemmons, in case you have forgotten, I'm taken." Emily watched Jack for a moment, attempting to assess what was happening between them. She loved Bill, of that she had no doubt. But in a few short hours, Jack had set her senses reeling, had her heart pounding, and introduced feelings that muddled her thinking.

"You know," Jack said, breaking the silence. "Twelve guests can live comfortably aboard *The Adamas*, and the crew is ready to take off anywhere in the world at a moment's notice."

"What are you trying to do, sell me a cruise?"

He laughed. "Not even close, I'm trying to sell you me."

Emily wasn't ready to admit Jack was irresistible. "On such a night with so charming a companion tearing at my sensibilities, I could easily surrender," she said playfully. "Unfortunately, unlike you, my circumstances don't allow me to sail off at a moment's notice."

"Are you making fun of me?"

She held up her thumb and forefinger. "Little bit. So what's the scoop, Jack?"

"I'm not entirely sure what you're getting at," answered Jack. "But here goes. Someone with no knowledge of the impact you're having on me, might suggest that I plan to impress you with my surroundings, and simply maneuver you into a sexual encounter."

"But you're not?"

"Not exactly…"

"How 'not exactly'?"

"Good grief, you certainly know how to put a guy on the spot."

"All part of my charm, dish."

"You're a genuinely interesting person, you've woven your way into my psyche, and I want so much more than sex from you."

Emily laughed. "Did you get that line off a crackerjack box?"

"Was it good? Did I convince you about the not-just-sex thing?"

Emily held up her thumb and finger again. "Little bit," she giggled. "But if you remember, I'm taken."

"I haven't forgotten," whispered Jack. "Don't you feel anything between us?"

Emily chewed on her lip. "How about we get more coffee and you tell me about your family."

"It's not a pretty subject."

"Everybody has a gross Uncle Morty in the closet. How bad can yours be?"

Jack smiled. "You know, Emily, I can't believe I feel so comfortable with you. We just met and I feel like I've known you all my life. What's that all about?"

"It doesn't have to be about anything. Sometimes it's simply two people becoming friends and getting together for dinner and a chat."

"Is that all we are?"

"I don't know you well enough to answer that."

Jack summoned the lounge waiter. "The hell with coffee. If I'm going to spill my guts, I need a brandy. You want some?"

"I'll have a sip of yours if that's okay."

Emily took a small sip when he handed her the snifter. "Our meeting is simply karma," she said. "An amusing cosmic event."

"Don't be flip," said Jack. "I'm serious. What sort of spell have you put on me?"

"I don't need a spell Jack. I might feel something too. But I can keep everything in perspective and not get carried away."

"I've wanted to carry you away from the minute I saw you."

"I know. Now tell me something really personal about yourself. Then, when you get me drunk and disabled, violate my person, and leave me spent and abandoned in the Kasbah, I can point the police directly at you."

"God, I really love your sense of humor."

Jack reached for her hand and she pulled it away.

"Tell me who you are, Jack Clemmons."

Chapter Two

Jack offered Emily the brandy but she declined more. Then he took a large swallow, and set the glass aside. "I'm the only child of Peter and Iona Clemmons of Walvis Bay, a small township on the Atlantic coast of west central Namibia in Africa. The settlement is about eleven hundred square kilometers and has a population of around forty-six thousand. Most of us can trace our families back to the eighteen hundreds, when Dutch colonists incorporated the bay into the Cape Colony."

"So your heritage is European, like mine. Yay, something in common. What do your folks do?"

"Walvis Bay's main claim to fame is a deep-water port, and my father is the major shareholder of the freight handling company that enables thousands of cargo ships to dock there. He also owns Walvis Bay Holdings, trading Namibian commodities like industrial diamonds, copper, gold, zinc, and uranium all over the world."

"So he's rich."

"Ridiculously."

"Ergo, so are you."

"Not so fast, my little gold-digging friend; let me tell you why that will probably never be." Jack took a swallow of brandy. "For some time, my father and other influential business leaders have been working to convince corporations to use our docks, instead of South Africa's further to the south. Their goal is to promote Walvis Bay and its commercial potential, and my no-brain useless job is to float around the world and select venues from which my father can host meetings and fancy parties for potential business partners. By bringing *The Adamas*, to Monaco, I get to be a glorified deckhand pandering to the ostentatious whims of the world's fat cat corporate vipers. In the coming month, I have the pleasure of remaining on hand to provide tour guide services to a parade of diamond dripping dowagers, while father convinces their husbands to part with their money."

"Yikes, that's some speech. Did I detect a smidge of anger in there?"

"Do you blame me?"

"So you're an events coordinator; it doesn't sound like a bad job to me. Try loading airline cargo for a living. Tell your father you're going to find a position you like better, somewhere else."

"It's not as simple as that."

"Tell him you're unhappy and need to find something that inspires you. He's your dad; surely he wants you to be happy and fulfilled."

"You'd think, but as he sees it, my life is an ongoing catalog of mistakes."

"We've all made mistakes."

"There you are," said Jack. "Spirit lifting again. You sure you're taken?"

"Positive. Now don't try and change the subject. Why don't you simply jump outside the box, go it alone and plunge into the unknown?"

"Would your parents trust you to plunge into the unknown?"

"I don't have any parents around to stop me. They died in a car accident when I was a kid. My grandmother raised me for a couple of years before she also died. Then I was sort of adopted by Jude, who is now my compulsive gambler roommate, and her companion Tina. It's funny; I found it strengthening to come from a place where I had to grow up fast. But I know the downside; it can make you feel very isolated."

"You don't seem to have a problem being outgoing."

"Believe me—until I met Bill, I was where you are. I once found it difficult to bare even a pinch of my soul. But when you find someone you can totally trust, and let all your angst out, things will fall into place."

"How'd you get so wise? What are you, all of twenty-five?"

"Twenty-eight," answered Emily. "What does your mother say about all this conflict?"

"Don't have a mother. Maybe none of this crap would have happened if I did."

"That's a real what-the-heck statement, what happened to her?"

"She and another couple were killed by elephant poachers while on safari. My father barely got out alive."

"No wonder he's overprotective."

"It's not that. He never cared about me. My mother was his only love and once she was gone, all he did was work. I was raised by a series of governesses and servants. Can you imagine what it's like to be surrounded by a bunch of people who only care about you because your father pays them?"

She squeezed his hand. "I can't begin to understand what you went through. All I can say is I've only known you a couple of days, and I care about you."

"Do you know how good it feels to hear someone say that?"

"Actually, I do. Now lose the blues." Emily looked at her watch. "Wow, look at the time. I've had a lovely time Jack. Dinner was yummy and your tour guiding was impeccable. But I have to get back to my room. Jude is probably pacing the floor wondering where I am."

"Will I see you again?"

Emily smiled. They had opened—and closed—a million Pandora's boxes. Had discussed politics, religion, and world affairs, and had compatibly set the world to rights with similar ideologies and irreverent humor. Philosophically, Jack appeared to be a younger version of Bill, and Emily found that revelation dangerously intoxicating. "As I said, you're a few years too late."

"It's never too late," whispered Jack. He was delighted he'd at last found a strong, intelligent woman who could hold her own on a dozen disparate subjects. And while she seemed reticent to delve too deeply into her personal life, he brushed any concern aside. Everyone was entitled to a few secrets. He certainly had his share. When he looked in her eyes, seeing honesty and sincerity went along with her beauty and intelligence. Whatever hers might be, he didn't care. And he couldn't let her simply disappear from his life. "Have dinner with me tomorrow. I'll show you the yacht."

"Open ocean with a man I just met…really?"

Jack put "scout fingers" to his temple. "No seriously, dinner and a boat ride. That's all, I swear."

"Let me think about it. Goodnight, Jack."

"At least let me walk you to your room."

Emily raised an eyebrow. "The elevator is it, buster."

As the doors closed, she watched his face. He had the look of an abandoned puppy.

Chapter Three

When Emily entered her room, it was clear Jude had not returned. It wasn't unusual for her roommate to disappear for days on end to gamble, so Emily tidied up the space and got ready for bed.

Surrounded by the cool permanence of The Hermitage's ancient marble bathroom, Emily took up a silver-backed hairbrush that had been her grandmother's and drew long sweeps through her chestnut hair. Her eyes closed, as she took pleasure from the relaxing strokes of the precious memento of happier times. But her mind was filled with confusion. Bill had shown his appreciation for her in a million ways, and showered her with affection and attention. Nevertheless, something intangible was always missing. Thoughts of Jack raced through her mind, and unexpected guilt flooded over her. *Had he displayed that intangible something?* Conflict threatened to overwhelm her, and as a barely perceptible draft wafted across her lashes, Emily opened her eyes. Her mother's face looked back from the mirror.

It wasn't the first time Cindy Wilks had appeared. She was always there when Emily had a crisis of conscience, although this time, she looked different. Her hazel eyes, familiar with gentle acquiescence, were gone, replaced by Emily's deep green. They were full of unquestionable determination, and her mother's small calm voice echoed uncharacteristically loud in her head. *What are you thinking? Bill isn't perfect, but he's the man for you. He can give you almost everything. Jack Clemmons is a flirtation. Don't give up what you have, for someone you barely know.*

Emily had never felt her mother's presence so intensely, or heard her message so clearly. No matter what, she could not see Jack Clemmons again. She pushed the sadness of her mother's loss into the remotest corner of her memory. And as the vision faded; Emily replaced the hairbrush in its case.

Chapter Four

Emily woke as the sun poured through the balcony window. Jude's bed had not been slept in, and she shook her head. *What now? How much has she lost, and how much is it going to cost?* Emily was fed up with Jude's gambling; fed up with the lies and deceit, and more than fed up helping someone who would never change out of tricky situations. However, as Emily climbed into the shower, she determined to put a positive spin on Jude's hopeless situation. Her mind was finally made up. As soon as she returned to America, she was putting Jude's nonsense behind her, and moving in with Bill.

Emily was dressed when she heard the key card in the door, followed by a cuss word. She knew it could only be Jude. And as her roommate stepped inside the room there was no mistaking she was mad.

"Don't say a fucking word," snapped Jude. "I lost all my money and now I'm leaving."

"Excuse me?"

"Shut up and get my ticket."

"We're wait-listed for tomorrow, remember? And what happened to your face?"

A purpled bruise and an angry welt accompanied a cut around Jude's eye. "Had an argument with somebody, and they might be waiting downstairs. Go get my ticket."

"First, tell me what happened."

"Don't want to talk about it," hissed Jude. "Just do as I say. Go get the goddamn ticket."

"Whoa, hang on; why are you mad at me?"

"I'm not. Get the fucking ticket."

"The flight is fully booked," said Emily calmly. "You won't get on today."

"I need to leave now. And I want some money for a cab."

"Money? Why do you want money? Surely you left some in the hotel safe."

"What word didn't you understand when I said 'I lost all my money'?"

"Oh my God, what did you do? Do you owe money now? Who did this to you?"

"Skip the inquisition, and move your ass."

"I knew this would happen if you went to the casino. Well tough luck, Jude, you're on your own. I'll get your ticket, but I'm through bailing you out."

As Emily headed for the door, Jude grabbed her arm, and viciously twisted it behind her back. "You ungrateful spoiled brat. All I want is cab fare to Nice airport. Now you've got two choices, either you give it willingly, or I'll beat it out of you."

Squirming from her grasp, Emily lurched toward the door, but Jude was too quick. She grabbed Emily's hair, pulled her back into the room, and spun her onto the bed.

"You crazy bitch," screamed Emily. "You've gone too far this time. I warned you what would happen if you hit me again. I'm calling the authorities."

Jude slapped Emily hard as she reached for the phone. "My, my, haven't you suddenly become Miss Upstanding Citizen. Now we have to change the plan." She ripped the phone wire from the wall. "It's obvious you can't be trusted so..." Jude turned, and dragged a suitcase from the closet. She threw it at Emily, grazing her face. "Get packing."

Emily felt a bump forming on her cheek bone. "Screw you, I'm not going anywhere. I'll give you the ticket and some money, and you can get the hell away from me."

"Too late for that; you're coming with me, if I have to drag you." Jude took a step toward the bed. "Besides you owe me."

"*Owe* you? Are you kidding? We had this conversation a dozen times. I'm done. I owe you nothing."

Jude's eyes glazed as she took hold of Emily's hair. "Who was it gave you shelter when your husband kicked you out? Who protected your lily-white ass after Bear Mountain? Who gave you money for drugs when you were selling your ass in the street?"

"That wasn't me," said Emily. "That was you and Tina. Look, none of what you're saying makes sense. You need help, let me call a doctor."

Emily attempted to stand, but Jude pushed her down and pulled a cigarette lighter from her pocket. Grabbing Emily's hair again, she flicked on the lighter and moved the flame closer. "What if I simply deal with you right now? Nobody will know. I can say it was an accident. You wanted a cigarette, the wind blew your hair and with too much hairspray, whoosh, up it went in a ball of flames."

Tears streamed down Emily's face. Jude was clearly unbalanced and in no state to reason. "Okay, Jude, whatever you say. We can sort this out. Let me go so I can pack. We'll go home, right now. Give me a few minutes."

As Jude backed off, Emily threw her things into the suitcase.

• • •

Within the hour Emily had retrieved her money and their tickets from the hotel's safety deposit box, and the pair made their way back to reception. Jude watched Emily closely, but she was able to scrawl "help, call the police" on the credit card receipt.

"Sorry, *mademoiselle*," said the desk clerk, pushing the receipt back toward Emily. "What might this say?"

"Er, it's a thank you...a thank you to the housekeepers," whispered Emily.

But Jude was within earshot, and after snatching the receipt, stood with her full weight on Emily's foot. "Sorry, our mistake," she said to the clerk. "Wrong amount for the tip, could you print us another receipt?" The desk clerk turned to the printer to pick up a new copy. "Do that again," Jude hissed, "and I'll kill you."

The receipt was produced, signed without further incident, and the women got in a cab to the Nice airport.

• • •

After several miles of tense silence, Jude put her hand on Emily's knee. "Why so quiet?" she said. "Aren't you glad to be going home?"

Emily slapped the hand away. "Shut up. I don't want to hear any of your crap right now."

"Maybe you'd rather I dropped you off here, and let your rich boyfriend rescue you."

"Anything would be preferable to listening to you."

"Is that so?" said Jude. "Well, maybe he'd like to hear what I have to say."

"There's nothing you could say about me that would bother him, so shut up."

"Oh, I think there is, Miss High and Mighty. Do his hoity-toity fat-cat family and friends know you're a lowly cargo bum taking him for every penny you can get? Might they be interested to know you were raised by a pair of drinking, gambling, drug-taking lesbians?"

"That's not the way it is, and you know it. Just shut up. I'm through with you."

"Are you indeed? Well maybe you'll feel better after talking to the police."

"Yes. That would be a good thing." Emily leaned forward to redirect the driver. "Let's stop the cab right now."

Jude's hand clamped onto Emily's knee, squeezing the bone so tightly pains shot from her ankle to thigh. "Not so fast Miss Innocent; let's review. What possible excuse could you come up with, for not reporting my involvement in that fatal accident, on Bear Mountain? How would you explain checks written from your bank account to drug dealers in Jackson Heights? Or—get this one—how would you justify talking to my contacts as I smuggled certain restricted commodities through the warehouse? And just to completely immerse you in the world of the unrighteous, I'm going to let you in on the score to end all scores when I get back to the States."

"Yeah, right," said Emily. "What are you going to do, rob a bank?"

"Better…I'm relieving good old Transcontinental of a zillion dollars' worth of diamonds."

Emily raised an eyebrow. "You're sick, and a truly certifiable idiot. It can't be done. You wouldn't get ten miles from the airport."

"My poor naive Emily. I told you. I have friends, and those friends have friends, and when the shit hits the fan, only you will be front and center with all manner of nasty things hanging over your head."

"You talk such a load of bullshit. Everybody knows nothing you say is true."

"And of course everybody knows what an innocent goody two shoes you are."

"I've never done anything illegal."

"Umm, now let's see. Your silence after the Bear Mountain incident, Jackson Heights drug dealer payoff." Jude was counting off on her fingers. "Accessory to smuggling—"

"I can explain all that."

"Well maybe you can. But in the meantime, you'll lose your job and your fancy friends, and let's see…all kinds of ugliness will happen to a pretty thing like you in prison."

"You'll get caught and lose everything, too."

"Na-ah. My friends have been covering my ass for some time and will continue to do it in the future." Jude smiled malevolently. "You must know sacrificing you would be nothing to them, or me, for that matter. So, unless you want the wrath of some very nasty people raining down on your head, I suggest you keep your trap shut, and do as you're told."

The contempt in Emily's eyes was impossible to hide.

"I know what you're thinking," Jude bent Emily's fingers painfully. "And let me tell you. You say one word to anyone, and I will drop you so deep in the shit a submarine couldn't get you out. Do you know what I mean?"

Emily snatched her hand free. "You need to be in an institution, you know that."

It was true she owed Jude. She and her partner Tina took her in when she had nowhere else to go, but that was years ago. And as Emily recalled those early days, understanding how circumstances had changed the dynamic of their relationship since, she knew it was now imperative she find a place of her own. Feeling obligated to Jude might have prevented her from moving on. But since Tina was killed, Jude's increasingly explosive outbursts were more than anyone could take. The awards dinner in Monaco had been a welcome opportunity to escape the tensions of living with so bitter a person. Now, as she stared blankly into the back of the seat in front of her, Emily could see no way out. She would do as she was told. She would keep quiet, and hope that like in times past, no one would discover the truth.

Chapter Five

Jack put down the phone and smiled. He always dreaded his father's calls, because they invariably ended with him having to apologize for forgetting to organize some nit-picking little social detail. However, it seemed Emily's spirit had not only bolstered his confidence on a personal level, but also prompted him to remember every tiny detail of Peter Clemmons 'must have' list.

He dialed The Hermitage to invite Emily to that evening's dinner party. However, when he asked to be put through to her room, Gaston, the guest services director told him Ms. Wilks had checked out.

"Do you remember her checking out?" Jack asked.

"But of course, she is normally a very beautiful woman."

"Normally?" cut in Jack.

"Why yes, *Monsieur* Clemmons. But this day it seemed she had befallen some accident for she had a large angry place down the side of her face."

Jack frowned. "Did she seem upset?"

"I am not qualified to judge such a thing, *monsieur*. But she seemed a little, er, agitated when she handed me the credit card receipt."

"Was she questioning the charges?" asked Jack.

"I don't think so. She had written something there, but it was so badly written I couldn't make it out. I asked her to translate and she said it was a thank you to the staff."

"How do you mean badly written?" asked Jack, who'd seen Emily's neat, precise penmanship.

"It was like my mother's writing and she has a shaky hand."

"Do you still have the receipt?" asked Jack.

"No, *monsieur*, the older women with her snatched it from my hand before I could staple it to the invoice."

"So where is your signed proof of payment?"

"I gave her another receipt," said Gaston.

"And this other woman; was there anything you remember about her?"

"*Mais oui, monsieur*. She was, excuse my bluntness, very masculine, and extremely angry about something. It might have had to do with the bruising and cuts on her face."

"They both had injuries?" asked a concerned Jack. "Good grief, Gaston, what on earth was going on? Did you register any reports of a disturbance in Ms. Wilk's room?"

"No, but it was Ferdinand who first brought the ladies' condition to my attention." Gaston handed the phone to the desk clerk. "Ferdinand, tell *Monsieur* Clemmons about the ladies' departure."

"When I brought down their suitcases, I remember *Mademoiselle* Wilks repeatedly asking the older woman why they were leaving," answered Ferdinand. "And she wanted to make a phone call, but was not allowed to do so. I assumed the older lady was irritated because the younger had them running late."

"Thank you, Ferdinand. You have been most helpful. Please put Gaston back on the phone."

"*Oui, monsieur.*"

"Gaston, I have to call and find out if Ms. Wilks is all right. Could you give me her address and phone number off the registration card?"

"For you, *monsieur*, yes. But it will be of little help. The address is simply listed as J.F.K. Airport, USA, and there is no phone number."

"Isn't that unusual?"

"Not for airline staff. If there are any problems, we simply bill the airline. However, the police authorities require a passport and full information upon entering Monaco. Maybe they can help?"

Jack might have accepted Emily's leaving as her choice had he not been told of her distressing appearance. Now, he had to find out what happened, and knew exactly who could help.

. . .

"Hello, Jack, old friend," said Chief Inspector Labande. "What can I do for you?"

"I know this is unorthodox, but could you let me have Emiline Wilks or Judith Cameron's complete address from the cards filled out when they entered Monaco?"

"That is not something we share with civilians, Jack. May I ask the reason you need such information?"

"Er…it's personal."

"*Naturellement*, go on."

"We—er, that is she, Ms. Wilks and I—are to be married," said Jack, resorting to a necessary lie. "I believe Ms. Cameron objects to our union and er, I think she may have taken my fiancée back to America to prevent our marriage."

"*Ah, mais oui*, a matter of the heart. We in Monaco understand such things. However, I am unable to help in this matter. All records are temporarily sealed while we investigate a murder along the waterfront."

"A murder," said a shocked Jack. "In Monaco?"

"It seems times are changing even in our little paradise. And since it is a rare occurrence, you understand how we must be very careful."

"Yes, of course, I understand. Any idea when you might be able to give me the information?"

"Who knows?"

"Charles, please; I know murder is a huge deal in Monaco, but all I want is one little address."

"It is out of my hands. I suggest you come back in a week."

"A week," said Jack. "That's an eternity. Couldn't I try again tomorrow?"

"Jack, I tell you this because we are friends. But after I tell you what we are doing, you will see how very busy we are, and why you cannot return for at least a week." Labande waited for some sort of confirmation that Jack agreed, but receiving no indication, he continued. "As you know, we have cameras everywhere in the Principality and can pinpoint any trouble outdoors. However, it appears our dead woman knew our system well. She was well known on the Cote d'Azure for discreetly picking up tourists and taking them back to her apartment to steal their money. We have been watching her for a while and had no cause to apprehend her. But now, with this messy business, we have to go back to our cameras and identify all the individuals with whom she had contact."

"You have the film. Surely it's a simple case of matching passport records. This is Monaco; stuff like this doesn't happen here. Why will it take a week to pull a few pictures?"

"As I said, times are changing. This type of thievery is more common than one might think. Naturally, it's not something we want to advertise; so very bad for Monaco's tourist reputation. However, when it happens, we have to look at mountains of security camera pictures and compare them to every passport and ID card we have, to see if a tourist or local is involved."

"Surely someone must have seen something. This is a small place with eyes everywhere."

"Just so, and right now we are closing in on one lead. A casino receptionist recognized the murder victim as being in the company of an American woman, to whom she passed a message on the night of the tragedy."

Jack interrupted. "Whoa, stop right there. You said an American who was given a message at the casino?"

"Yes," said Labande. "The message was relayed as her passport was being photographed."

"That's my friend. Well, not my friend. My friend's friend. She sent the message. It was her friend. The friend of the one I'm looking for."

"Jack, slow down, you are making no sense; whose friend did what? Look, you need to come down to police headquarters. Do you want me to send a car for you?"

• • •

Within the hour, Jack was with the Inspector of Records, in front of a computer displaying all the information he required. Armed with everything he needed and oblivious to the bigger picture, Jack was eager to contact Emily. He turned to leave, but Labande blocked the door.

"No no, Jack, you cannot simply leave. You are now part of an ongoing murder investigation, and you must do nothing to jeopardize it. You will need to give statements, and you cannot contact Mademoiselle Wilks, as she may alert Judith Cameron."

"Emily wouldn't say anything," Jack snapped. "Besides, she could be in danger. Gaston at The Hermitage told me she had bruises on her face."

"In that case," interrupted Labande. "It is even more important you do nothing to interfere. If this Judith Cameron killed the Dutch woman, and afterwards beat your friend, she is very dangerous. Mademoiselle Wilks may be in fear and who knows what she might say to protect herself from another beating. You will say and do nothing, and you will not leave Monaco until I give you permission." Jack began to protest, but was quieted. "You must give me your word you will do nothing to contact Emiline

Wilks. If our investigation is damaged by your interference, our friendship will mean nothing, I will arrest you as an accessory. Do I make myself clear?"

Jack nodded sheepishly. "Who will protect Emily? Don't you see the Cameron woman forced her to leave the Principality? I knew she wouldn't leave willingly without saying goodbye."

"Jack, I'm sorry, but this is the way it must be. I will contact the FBI and other American authorities and they will protect your friend if she is innocent."

"What do you mean, *if* she is innocent? Of course she is innocent. She was with me on the evening of the murder."

"I understand what you say and we will need to hear more about that. Come with me now, and I will take a full statement. But make no mistake, once that is done and you leave here, I will be checking on your whereabouts. You may not leave the Principality until I tell you, and if you try to leave, it will be very bad for you."

Chapter Six

Jack was frantic. He imagined all manner of dire things happening to Emily at the hands of Jude Cameron. But he was powerless to help. He decided to let a large brandy persuade him that he was overreacting to a situation about which he knew nothing. And when one drink nowhere near calmed his fears, he took another. And then another ...

• • •

When Jack awoke, head ready to burst and eyes glued half shut, he felt a presence beside him. "Who's that…where am I?"

"It's Tom, sir; you're in your cabin."

Jack felt his pajama-clad chest. "Christ, what happened?"

"You had a brandy or two, sir." The steward engaged the intercom. "Captain said I should buzz him when you woke."

"Okay, can I get some coffee?"

"Right away."

As the steward left, Captain Kris Svensson walked in. "So, Jack," he said, towering over the bed. "I guess this is about the young lady you had dinner with."

"Don't start, Kris."

"I'm not here to judge; your father does plenty of that. Just thought you might want to talk about it. Maybe this old Norseman can impart some ancient wisdom."

"Got anything for a hangover?"

"I'm told goose grease on stale bread works." The Captain smiled when Jack made a face. "Not for you, uh? How about a raw egg in Worcestershire sauce?"

"Thanks, but no thanks. I'll pass on both."

"So what happened?"

Jack ran a hand through his hair. "How long have I been out?"

"About ten hours," said the Captain. "I was going to give you twelve before calling the morgue."

"Very funny, old man."

"Not so funny. It'd be my hide if anything happened to you."

"No, it wouldn't. My father doesn't give a shit about what happens to me."

Captain Svensson sat. "But I do. What happened with you and…?"

Jack pushed his knuckles into his throbbing temples. "Emily, and why do you assume it's about her?"

"Because the last time you got this upset was after you found out that gal in New Zealand was married."

"Well, you're dead wrong; nobody's married."

"Let me finish. I know it's about her because Tom told me you asked her aboard but when you called the hotel, she'd checked out."

"Jesus, is nothing sacred aboard this rust bucket?"

"Hey, be careful what you say about the woman I love."

Jack walked to the porthole, opened it and let the cool sea breeze wash over him. "At least she won't run out on you."

"That's it, then…she left you high and dry?"

"Story of my life." Jack forced a smile. "You didn't put these God-awful pajamas on me, did you?"

"What do you think?"

"Thanks, Kris, I can always count on you."

"As long as you remember that. Now, as you're relatively okay, I'll get back to work. Why don't you get up on deck? The fresh air will do you good, clear out the cobwebs, and put it all in perspective."

"That's what Emily said, 'I can keep everything in perspective and not get carried away'."

"Sounds like she's committed to someone else," said the Captain.

"Why do you assume that?"

"I'm an old sea dog, Jack. That's the sort of line a gal uses when she wants to let you down lightly. You have to suck it up and move on."

"I don't think I can do that. Gaston at The Hermitage said she was beaten up before she left."

"By whom?"

"They think her roommate."

"Then the police need to get involved."

"They already are."

"Good grief, Jack, what have you gotten into?"

"Nothing, but her life seems a bit messy."

Captain Svensson stood and headed for the door. "Look, sober up and we'll talk again. If you need help, I'll be there."

"Fank u mommy; I weerwy wuv you."

"Cut the crap, kid; just do as your Captain orders."

• • •

Jack's head was pounding fit to explode, but when he opened the bathroom cabinet looking for something to make it stop, he found nothing. Then he heard the door. "Thank God," he said, reaching for coffee.

Tom held up a glass containing a dubious slimy brown and yellow mixture. "Captain said you should chug this first."

"What is it?"

Tom raised an eyebrow. "Prairie oyster. Thought everyone knew about these. Looks disgusting, but really works."

"Personal experience, Tom?"

"Yes, sir."

"Then I'll do it." Jack rolled the concoction of raw egg and Worcestershire sauce in the glass and being at a pain-point where he'd try anything, chugged it down. "Eeeuw, that's worse than shit-on-a-shingle."

Tom looked puzzled. "I like shit-on-a-shingle."

"That's because you're ex-military; they make you eat anything."

"Don't you know it. Next, Captain says you have to take a cold shower with the water full flowing on your head."

"You're kidding, right?"

"Wouldn't joke about something like that. Got my reputation as Tommy-on-the-spot to think about."

"Can I at least have a mouthful of coffee to wash away the goop?"

"No, sir. Shower first, then coffee. I brought toast, too. Captain's orders."

"Please don't tell me it has goose grease on it."

Tom looked puzzled. "Excuse me?"

"Nothing. I'll hit the shower."

. . .

Ten minutes of water-induced brain freeze had Jack's headache gone. Moreover, the prairie oyster had calmed his nausea. And, as he sat on the roof deck, with fresh sea air drifting over him, he was ready to face the day.

Tom brought Jack's breakfast and the newspapers. "Chef made your favorite frittata, sir."

"Tell him thank you; I appreciate how much you all do for me." Jack hesitated.

"Was there something else you need?" asked Tom.

"I don't suppose any messages came in for me?"

"Stopped by Sparkie before I came up, sir. Nothing received."

"Thanks, Tom." Jack's crestfallen look spoke volumes. "Thanks for checking."

• • •

In the beginning, Jack had been confident Emily would contact him. However, a week passed with no word from her. Try as he might, he couldn't dismiss her as merely a flirtation, because everything about her was different. He couldn't begin to quantify the depth of feelings produced by their short time together, and he desperately missed her conversation and infectious spirit. And when the hurt of her departure morphed into something more desperate, he obsessed about her welfare. No matter what, he intended to find out what happened to her.

• • •

Agonizing days passed and with the arrival of Peter Clemmons guests, Jack resigned himself to further purgatory playing the dutiful son of the host. He accompanied one or the other of the guest's offspring to local events, and while he tried to be marginally attentive, Jack constantly compared the women to Emily. He found both lacking.

And when a champagne-fueled Katarina—the more aggressive of the two—made a pass at Jack; he simply smiled. There was no doubt she was rich and beautiful and, at least in his father's eyes, would make a suitable wife.

But the vapid young woman reminded Jack of his first sexual partner at university. Had he still been that young and shallow, he might have been flattered and taken the young woman to his bed. As it was, he didn't even care enough about her, to care. His sustaining force was recalling his time with Emily.

Chapter Seven

Jack eventually reached a point where he wanted to leave Monaco and accept any consequences the authorities might levy. Then common sense kicked in. The ramifications of so blatant a defiance might keep him from Emily longer. So, he elected to go to police headquarters and plead with Labande to let him leave. This time he was successful. But not before Labande had told him all he could about the murder.

•••

Chief Inspector Labande dropped sugar into his fourth cup of coffee, and sucked the dregs from the stir stick. He'd been having a hard time with the details of the Dutch girl's murder. Now, as he sat in front of his computer screen, message ready to send, the thought his friend Jack might become involved added more gray to his already salt and pepper hair.

Sipping his coffee, he glanced from the window. Monegasques were diligently going about their business. Happy, smiling people were spilling from the recently docked cruise ships, and the majestic Grimaldi Palace rose undisturbed and stately from the water. Labande frowned. He liked living in a place where murder was still rare; a place where such disgusting callousness could only be the work of an outsider with a sick and demented mind.

As he flipped through the crime scene pictures, he wondered what kind of jaded personality could have abandoned a paralyzed and bleeding girl. And the forensic evidence was clear. The Dutch girl fell, gashed the back of her head on the edge of a coffee table, and injured her spine enough to incapacitate her. And while someone else had been in the apartment during that time, they left her to die.

Labande looked more closely at certain photographs. One showed the victim had attempted to write her killer's name in blood. Another, where the young woman was a blue-grey mass of contortion, bled out at the end of a dragging crimson trail. She had died a slow horrible death and Labande couldn't help thinking how it was all such a pitiful waste. But what was worse, and made his hand shake with thinly veiled anger; given immediate medical attention, Ms. Marisa Marten would have survived her trauma.

Now, as he opened the file sent him by the FBI, the Monegasque policeman put their, and his, pieces together. The pieces that started to make sense by accident, as so many cases do. He'd been looking over the international flight watches and had seen Judith Cameron's name as being a person of interest in an illegal currency transaction in Switzerland. Cameron, an American, had exchanged a large amount of Swiss francs at the casino. And in replying to the FBI alert, Labande informed them he had reason to believe his murder case and Cameron were connected. Cameron, who roomed at The Hermitage with Emiline Wilks, the woman his friend Jack Clemmons, was so frantic to contact.

Labande frowned. Good, trusted friends were hard to come by. Nevertheless, while Jack Clemmons might have nothing to do with either case, his fiancée was on the periphery of both.

The last mouthful of coffee ran bitter over Labande's tongue. And as he vowed to cut down on the caffeine-infused beverage, he hit the send key informing the FBI of Jack Clemmons arrival.

• • •

When *The Adamas'* group assembled for dinner that evening, Peter Clemmons misinterpreted his son's demeanor.

"Well," Peter said to the assembly. "It seems escorting a pair of eligible young ladies agrees with my son. Do I detect an understanding in our midst?"

Jack smiled. "An understanding, Father; how quaint."

"Maybe, but you appear different this evening; cheerful and seemingly full of optimism. I hear you've been spending an inordinate amount of time with our beautiful Katarina. Do we have cause for celebration?"

"I don't believe I've spent any more time with Katarina than with Sarah. But you're right, an announcement is indeed forthcoming."

Katarina fidgeted in her seat. "Jack, I had no idea; you seemed so taciturn."

"Taciturn? Good for you, Katarina. Nothing says wasted education like dropping a ten dollar word when a one dollar word would clearly do."

Peter Clemmons' eyes flashed. "Jack, mind your manners; what's gotten into you?"

"Life, Father. Mind-clarifying, soul-boosting life. And for once, I'm going to live it on my terms."

"What the devil does that mean?"

"Tomorrow, come hell or high water, I'm leaving for America."

"You can't simply—"

Jack stood and threw down his napkin. "Watch me."

• • •

Jack rose early the following morning and was surprised to find his father already on *The Adamas'* upper deck. "You want more coffee, Father?"

"I'm good, but I'll take some fruit."

Jack spooned a measure into a bowl and set it beside his father.

"You not eating?" Peter Clemmons asked.

"Not hungry."

"That's not like you. Are you sick?"

"Sick of this place."

Peter bent down the corner of his newspaper. "Really?"

"Yes, really."

"So you're determined to go to America."

"This afternoon."

Peter Clemmons laid down his newspaper. "For what?"

"Business."

"Are you going to the diamond cutters expo?"

"No," answered Jack.

"Then what?"

"My business."

The elder Clemmons raised an eyebrow. "You have business?"

"That's what I said."

"And where are you staying?"

Jack shrugged. "Like New York isn't awash with suitable hotel rooms."

"Sarcasm. Well, that's new. Your little girlfriend teach you that?"

"How do you know about—?"

"Does it matter? Let's just say I have people who are keeping an eye on you."

Jack poured himself more coffee. "So, you know better than to refer to her as my little girlfriend. She's important to me."

"They always are."

Jack scowled. "Who always are?"

"Gold diggers."

"Christ, Father, could you for once not assume—it doesn't matter what you think, I'm going."

"I know." Peter Clemmons pulled a paper from beneath his plate. "So rather than have you mugged and left in an alley somewhere, I suggest you contact any of these people." He handed Jack a list. "You'll not need to bother about hotels. These are respectable families, who've had experience keeping wayward offspring out of mischief."

Exasperated, but knowing better than to argue the point with his father, Jack accepted the list and set his mind on New York.

Chapter Eight

It was six A.M. when Emily's cab pulled up to the glass-fronted reception of JFK's Executive handling area. She could see Bill's pilot, Joe, coffee in hand, chatting with the prettiest girl in the office. Waving hello, she went straight to the helicopter, and strapped in. She and Jude were on opposite shifts at Transcontinental, and on days off Emily put as much distance between them as possible. And while a pang of guilt for leaving Jack so abruptly occasionally tore at her heart, she knew that deciding to live with Bill was the right decision.

It was a couple of minutes before a smiling Joe appeared, handed her a headset, and received clearance to cross JFK's airspace.

"So?" asked Emily, no longer hearing instructions from the tower.

Joe turned and beamed. "So what?"

"Don't play coy, fly-boy; did you ask her out?"

Joe remained silent.

"Not again. Come on, what are you waiting for? It's been months."

Joe blushed beneath his headset. "I know, but she's sort of shy, and I didn't want to push it. She lives in Queens, I live in Saratoga. You know the deal."

"Duh! I do know the deal, and it's nothing. Bill said you could use the helicopter anytime. You have to come down to pick me up every week, so come up the night before, take her out, then fly me back to Harrington the next day. Why are you hesitating?"

"I suppose I could do that, but—"

"But nothing, you're just a big wimpy doofus. She's a really nice girl, and I think you should jump in, before someone beats you to it. Promise when you bring me back, if she's on duty, you'll ask her out"

"I'm not sure."

"Come on, promise. Stop being a wuss. One date, that's all. It's not like you're asking her to marry you."

"Whoa," said an alarmed Joe. "Don't even go there. That's a bad, bad word."

"Uh-oh, touched a nerve, eh?"

"Eh, nothing, I'll think about it."

"No thinking, stop thinking, too much thinking, just do it. What's the matter with you? You're good looking, you have a great job, and you get paid oodles—"

"Hey," he said pointing down. "Look at that development, what would you say? Mill and a quarter each, what do you think?'

"Stop trying to change the subject. I'm keeping on you about this. You'd be so sweet together; Joey and Jilly, a perfect match. Ask her."

"Just quit it, sister; you're not the boss of me."

Emily smiled. "Well technically, when you're not with Bill, I am."

"Yes, you are. But I still control the bird…" With that, Joe plunged the helicopter downward.

Emily shrieked. "Stop that, you monster, or I'll throw up on your boots."

Joe laughed at Emily's discomfort. "You gonna stop playing big sister?"

"Okay, okay, let's just get home safe."

• • •

They were thirty minutes into the journey, when Joe reached into the pocket of his flight suit, and handed Emily a small package "From Bill."

She smiled. "Naturally." Carefully untying the gold ribbon, Emily meticulously stowed the wrapping paper in the console pocket.

"Thanks," said Joe, grinning. "Never know when I might need some wrapping paper."

Emily ignored him, and upending a familiar Tiffany blue box, dropped a small turquoise pouch into her hand. Exploring the velvety depths, she pulled out a gold chain on which hung a heart-shaped deep-green emerald.

Joe was grinning like a schoolboy delivering his best friend's first love letter. "So what does it say?"

"What does what say?"

"You know damn well…The card?"

"Didn't you read it already?"

"Certainly not," said Joe. "It's private."

"Then I'm not telling you; it's private."

"To match your eyes."

Emily backhanded him. "You did look. Oh, you are such a boy."

"Am not, smarty pants. Bill discussed it with me when we chose it."

"And what else did you boys discuss?"

"Nothing…"

"Liar!"

•••

When the skids hit the west lawn of Harrington Hall, Bill's rambunctious Labradors bounded up to greet her. Dropping to her knees, she received the onslaught of wet kisses, and producing three Bonz from her shoulder bag, gave each a cookie.

Jeff, the houseman, was waiting and took Emily's case.

"Is Mr. Bailey playing golf?" she asked him.

"Yes Miss, said I was to take you straight over when you got in."

Emily smiled. Bill always liked to see her as soon as she arrived. And whether he was in a meeting or playing golf with his friends, everything stopped for her. He'd never admitted it, but Emily had a sneaking suspicion her interruption was a blessed relief. Bill was an excellent sportsman in general, but was horribly bad at golf.

Emily followed Jeff to the estate run-about. "Can you stop at the house for a minute, I have to do something."

"Sure Miss Emily, take your time. It will give Mr. Bailey a chance to get out the bunker."

• • •

As Emily passed the morning room, a picture of her loomed large above the fireplace. Over the years, Bill had taught her a lot about art and the foibles of the rich and privileged, but she'd never quite understood why that picture gave him such comfort. She couldn't help smiling as she trotted up the stairs. He was without doubt the most generous person she had ever known, and never for one second gave her any less than one hundred percent of himself. And then Jack popped into her mind, and she regretted not making a greater effort to say goodbye to him. She'd felt the sting of abandonment in her life and it wasn't something she would wish on anybody. However, with Jude threatening to expose the skeletons in her life, Emily knew it was best she get back to her routine with Bill. Besides, any apology she might tender to Jack would now be too little, too late.

• • •

Emily watched as Bill drove a ball high over the left side of the fairway that soundly smacked the uppermost branches of a very inconveniently placed tree. As it disappeared into the rough, a well-used curse floated across the distance.

Emily applauded as Bill handed his caddy the club. "Bravo, sir," she teased. "Fine use of obstacles."

Bill turned, smiling wide, all thoughts of golf abandoned. "How long have you been there?"

"Long enough to know you need a break."

"Whoa, and what's with the black eye?" he asked, kissing her carefully.

"The peril of a crowded flight. Some doofus had stuffed a huge bag into the overhead locker and when I opened it to get a book, damn thing fell out and hit me in the face. Don't worry, it looks a lot worse than it is."

"As long as you're okay."

"I am very okay, and you will find that out in a few minutes."

It was no secret to Bill's friends, and certainly not to his servants, that the things he and Emily did kept him young. Moreover, as Emily smiled at him, fresh as a daisy in a white pleated skirt and sunshine-yellow top, his golf buddies understood he was about to embark on a game, any one of them would much rather play.

"Carry on, guys," Bill said. "Play through and we'll see you later for drinks. Emily and I have business to discuss."

His friends smiled knowingly, and resumed their game.

As Jeff moved to the back seat of the estate run-about, Bill joined Emily on the bench-seat up front. And as he slipped the truck in gear, Emily moved in close and whispered what they might do with their afternoon. One intriguingly breathless proposal prompted Bill to run his hand high up Emily's thigh. She wasn't wearing panties, and he smiled broadly. "My, my Miss Wilks," he said, removing his hand. "If you want us in the ditch, just keep making those smutty suggestions."

She squirmed seductively closer and blew in his ear.

Bill did his best to drive a straight course. "No fair. Now back off, or I'll stop this truck and commit despicable acts upon your person in front of Jeff."

With no windows save the windshield, Jeff couldn't avoid hearing what the lovers were saying. "'Scuse me for saying, Mr. Bailey, but the wife told me I wasn't to get my blood pressure up. If it's all right with you, would you drop me off before the despicable acts occur?"

"Why, Jeff," said Emily facing the rear. "I do believe we've embarrassed you."

Jeff beamed. "Not a bit of it, Miss. It's just that when I tell the missus what I witnessed, she might want some of them despicable acts herself."

They all laughed as the truck chugged back to the house.

• • •

As soon as the truck came to rest at the Hall's front steps, Emily jumped out, and dragged Bill unceremoniously into the foyer, and up the grand staircase. In passing, she shouted to Brothers, Harrington's butler of twenty-five years, to bring champagne.

The spry old retainer smiled knowingly and headed off to the kitchen.

Brothers had always been in service, and sometimes found it difficult to accept the more relaxed relationships of the American household. Nevertheless, while ostensibly Bill's butler, he could maintain an appropriate distance, and still be a confidante, and friend. Being so close to Bill, he often speculated why Emily didn't stay at the Hall permanently as Bill had so many times requested. He assumed she wanted to 'do her own thing', and while he wasn't sure what that meant; he admired her independence. Brothers was also a co-conspirator in most of the surprises Bill planned for Emily. He also knew that while the world was hers for the asking, she had never asked Bill for anything. However, what most endeared Emily to those who lived and worked at Harrington was her joyful presence. She brought the place to life, and her antics were a continuing source of respectful amusement below stairs.

•••

Within minutes of collecting champagne and canapés, Brothers was knocking on the door to the master suite. Bill and Emily were in the bedroom, he on an oversized mahogany chair, she straddling his lap. Brothers placed the tray on the sitting room table, and quickly retreated. To the casual observer, the lovers appeared to be fully clothed, but without underwear to inhibit her, Emily was performing an almost imperceptible lap dance on Bill, which she'd suspended upon Brothers arrival. However, as soon as the outer door closed, Emily peeled off her top, revealing the stunning emerald pendent nestled between her breasts. And while Bill subconsciously compared its color to her eyes, her rhythmic rocking intensified and stripped the years from his body.

•••

It was in the quiet minutes after lovemaking that Emily worried about Bill. He always kept pace with her antics, but as they lay close, she worried that his heart beat dangerously fast.

"Darling," she whispered. "Can I ask you a question?"

"How am I feeling? I'm good. I don't know why these quiet moments bother you so much."

"That's all you know, smarty pants. That wasn't my question."

"Then fire away."

"When we met in Fiji, did you find me instantly attractive?"

"It's not like you to fish for a compliment," said Bill. "What brought this on?"

"Something somebody said to me in Monaco."

"Ah, the awards dinner; how did it go?"

"I didn't win the diamond tennis bracelet."

"I know you don't really give a toss about jewelry, so do I need to worry about us?"

Emily pecked him on the cheek. "Absolutely not."

"I think you know how I felt about you from minute one."

"Is that normal for a guy?"

"Being honest, I'd have to say yes. Of course it's all testosterone driven at first. We get a singular urge for sex, but if the couple is right together, other feelings take over. So, what happened in Monaco? Do I need to put a guard on you?"

"No. In fact the conversation clarified some stuff, and from now on you'll be seeing a lot more of me."

"Excuse me?"

"You still want a roommate?"

Bill beamed. "You'll marry me?"

Emily ran her fingers down his cheek. "Let's take one step at a time and live together. But at some point, when you least expect it, I promise to drag you in front of a Justice of the Peace and make a gentleman out of you."

"Deal," whispered Bill, before he locked his mouth on hers.

Chapter Nine

Bill and Emily's friends, among Saratoga's wealthiest, were assembled in the conservatory for their pre-race-day buffet breakfast. Upon asking, Emily was told Bill was taking a phone call in his office.

"Well, here we are again," said Emily, to her assembled friends. "Brad, would you be a dear and pass me a cup of coffee."

As Brad handed it to her, he ushered her aside. "Emily, love, I don't mean to be a downer, but is Bill okay?"

"Why do you ask?"

"Nothing really I suppose. But he's been looking a little peaked lately, and twice during the week, he begged off our golf game."

Emily smiled. "I wouldn't read too much into that." She patted Brad's ample belly. "You know he only plays to get you fat cats out for some exercise. Besides, he really isn't very good at it and you know Bill hates not being good at something."

"You got that right. His doctor appointment in New York went well then? Guess it's wishful thinking on my part that the old boy is actually slowing down."

"Umm." Emily paused. "Now go check out the buffet, and stop fretting. I bet we have smoked salmon thingies."

Brad smiled. "I love the thingies."

"That's why I asked cook to make extra."

As Brad disappeared, Emily might have seemed calm, but the slowing down remark got her thinking. It was universally understood Bill had the constitution of a horse, and was never sick. So, it was unusual for one of his closest friends to ask after his health. And the doctor appointment set off alarm bells in her head. Bill never visited the city without inviting her to spend the night with him at the Pierre. Emily excused herself and joined Bill in his study.

When Bill saw Emily, his face lit up. He made a beeline for her and kissed her passionately. "You look ravishing, I could eat you."

Emily giggled. "I think the good Reverend Ballard might have something to say about that. What are you doing in here? We have guests."

"Had a phone call and some urgent papers."

"Shall I make your excuses? The gang can see you later at the track."

"All done. Anyway you know my time is your time, no exceptions." Bill picked up a piece of paper and held it aloft, as if it were a proclamation. "Says right here in rule twenty-seven, sub-section five, paragraph three. And…er…b, clearly states, 'when Ms. Emily Wilks is present, no further business, save that of gaming, partying and fornication shall be conducted'."

"Fornication?"

Bill smiled. "Best I could do on short notice. Come here, I need some serious sugar." He came from behind the desk, enveloped her possessively in his arms, and kissed her hungrily.

It was several seconds before they separated. "Wow," said Emily. "Where did that come from?" Emily pulled back and looked deep into his eyes. "What's wrong, Bill?"

"Why would you think something is wrong?"

"What's all this…" She circled a finger in the air, not knowing how to describe what she felt from him.

Since they first met, Bill had taken great pains to shelter her from anything difficult. Now, he sat on the edge of the desk, pulled Emily between his legs, and buried his head in her shoulder.

The neediness in Bill's demeanor was something she'd never experienced before. "Seriously, darling, this doesn't feel right; what's happening?"

"Nothing really. I've had a hellish week since you left. I'm so relieved you came back."

"Why would you doubt I'd be back?"

Bill rarely alluded to negativity, and when he saw the look of concern on Emily's face, he smiled. "It's nothing but lonely old man stuff."

"Somebody said you'd seen the doctor."

"Routine physical."

"In New York?"

"Yeah, Doc Mathers."

Emily frowned. "He's not your regular. What gives?"

"Man stuff."

"I'll take that as 'I don't want to talk about it'."

"Do you mind?"

"Not for now, because we have a roomful of our friends waiting, and frankly, I think you'll feel a lot better after you've eaten some breakfast. But I won't forget to ask you later."

"What would I do without you?" asked Bill. "You know me better than I know myself. Everything is so much easier when you're here with me."

There was no doubt in Emily's mind that Bill loved her, and despite the limitations of his age, on so many levels, she loved him, too. And when she looked deep into his eyes, she also knew she had no right to play games with such a gentle, wonderful man any longer.

"All this old body needs is a dose of Emily," said Bill.

"Well unfortunately we have an obligation that requires our immediate presence. But I promise you will have my undivided attention after the races."

Emily started for the door, but Bill pulled her to a halt and pecked her on the nose. "I've been waiting a week for someone to tell me that."

"Good, so let's go attack the buffet, I'm hungry."

As Emily led Bill into the breakfast room, Brothers stepped to her side. "If you would like to sit, Miss Emily," he said. "I'll serve breakfast."

"Serve breakfast? This is Harrington Hall; we work under British rule. You never *serve* breakfast."

Brothers grinned as he turned to the buffet. Bill sat Emily at the head of the breakfast table.

"Okay, what's going on?" she said.

With a flourish, Brothers placed a covered plate before her. "Your breakfast, Miss…" He lifted the lid exposing a glass of orange juice. And all around, sparkling with more carats than anyone had a right to receive was a diamond necklace, tennis bracelet and matching earrings. "Mr. Bailey thought you might enjoy some ice with your O.J."

Emily was speechless.

"Assembled friends," said Bill, hoisting a glass of Bollinger. "Once again, I fell short of marriage, but finally, Emily has agreed to live here permanently. Please raise your glasses to 'the almost Mrs. Bailey'."

As Bill beamed like a Cheshire cat, and their closest friends cheered, Emily had no doubt she had made the right decision.

• • •

A happy, somewhat tipsy group set off for the races, and as he got into the limo, Bill instructed Brothers to break out champagne for everyone below stairs. Then the caravan of expensive automobiles snaked its way to the Saratoga Race Track.

"Why do you spoil me rotten," Emily asked, twirling the tennis bracelet beside the gold Rolex he'd bought her three years before. "I don't deserve all these beautiful things."

Bill watched her fidget with her wrist. "You sounded genuinely disappointed about not winning the tennis bracelet in Monaco.

and that's not like you. So I figured, umm, maybe my frugal little butterfly has changed her mind about jewelry. So let's blow her mind with something sparkly."

"You're crazy, you know that."

Bill pecked her on the nose. "Crazy about you. Does it fit? I can have it sized if it bothers you."

"Are you kidding? You know the exact size of every inch of my body." She moved her hand inside his thigh. "And I know yours."

Her remark was so spontaneous, so wickedly cheeky, so very Emily, Bill roared. "We can turn the car around and spend the day in bed if you prefer. I'd like to see you naked except for the diamonds."

"Very tempting Mr. Bailey, but you dragged your friends out of bed at the crack of dawn. The least we can do is ply them with champagne and munchies until the final race."

"You say you don't deserve my gifts, but there you go again, thinking about others. That's what makes you so deserving." He brushed her knuckles with his lips. "I'm going to spend the rest of my life spoiling you."

Chapter Ten

It was a perfect fall day for racing with the going recorded as 'good to soft'. The main event was the 'Travers Cup', a mile-and-a-quarter for three-year olds, and the grandstand, private boxes, turf terrace and rail pavilion were packed. Many of Bill and Emily's friends were in his box, though a few had chosen to go down to rail side. They were now waving like lunatics, gesturing for Emily to join them. Bill urged her to go and experience the excitement of the race at eye level, but the crowd was too intense for her.

As the horses spilled onto the course for the running of the Travers, the crowd noise was deafening. One not familiar with the tangible ego of the horse might think the racket would spook them, but the highly-strung equine athletes thrived on the noise. They fed off it like a band at a rock concert, and the horses pranced, twirled, and fitfully jogged to the start. There they were met by a necessarily burly course crew, whose unenviable task it was, to squish each of the gyrating powerhouses into the starting gate.

As expected, Jamie Freestone's Shirley Girley was odds-on favorite, and not worth a bet. However, Bill liked the look of his friend Josh's Anything Goes, while Emily chose to support Amy Salt's Pocket Rocket.

The crowd grew quiet as each horse melded into its starting stall. Then, exercising the prerogative to be loaded last, the favorite was coaxed into place. In the time it took to stall Shirley Girley the rest of the field became antsy, and several jockey's voices were heard calming their mounts. Then, when the favorite attempted to rear in position, her jockey slapped her smartly to settle her down.

As the hush of rapt anticipation descended over the track, the favorite again launched skyward. And as Shirley Girley's hooves hovered over the turf, a hollow metallic clang accompanied the crowd's universal gasp. The gates were open. Ears forward, equine timing impeccable, the mare powered from her haunches and hurtled from the stall.

Supporting yells from the crowd helped the horses into their strides, and the field bunched tightly together over the first couple of furlongs. No jockey was willing to make a break. And as the stampede approached the stands and the crowd noise increased, the horses surged forward. Relishing the encouragement, jockeys added their voices, and galloped hard to the turn. The front-runners jostled for position on the rails and settled. However, they re-bunched dangerously around the first corner, travelling at a faster pace than expected. The bumping and boring resulted in a rank outsider, Blue Bayou, breaking away from the pack. Some of the following jockeys anticipated an opening, and spread. But it was quickly apparent when Blue Bayou's jockey looked back, that he had set her into a pounding rhythm, to try and outrun the field. For several seconds nobody broke away to keep up, and although a mile-and-a-quarter, flat-out, was a long way to go; it looked like Blue Bayou might run away with it.

By the second turn, the blue roan had a commanding lead, and with her pace strong and steady, her jockey did little more than let her run. However, when he looked back a second time, the others were gaining. He attempted to chivy her on. And while the third turn saw a marked reduction in her lead, she still cleared the mile marker first. Then, as if she were standing still, others were on her shoulder. Slapping her once on the rump, her jockey tried to maintain speed. But the punishing pace and early break, proved too much for the youngster. As the field favorites passed Blue Bayou, she had given everything she had.

A tight group charged down the final two furlongs. Jockey experience, as well as the horse's stamina, would now come into play. Anything Goes took the lead, and within half a dozen strides, maintaining the blistering pace were Happy Go Lucky, Shirley Girley, and Pocket Rocket.

Whips cracking and heads down, the last furlong saw three jockeys glaring at each other as they rode neck and neck. Anything Goes hugged the rail. Happy Go Lucky was pinned in the middle. Shirley Girley set the pace, on the outside. Stride for stride, the three-year-olds charged on. With the finish in sight, adrenaline powered muscles flexed to the limit. And jockeys drove their mounts harder. With the crowd cacophony deafening, jockeys cursed and whips flailed. The equine trio responded. As hooves flashed close together, inches separated the runners from total disaster. Necks stretched, ears back, and nostrils spread, thoroughbred heads pushed free, and three horses shared the lead. Shoulder to shoulder, then neck and neck, Shirley Girley inched forward. Then nose, and nose, with relentless power, and equine determination, the favorite made her move. She was a sweating, foaming freight train, a hurtling mass of horseflesh, and when her jockey let out a blood-curdling scream, even he was surprised by her turn of speed. Shirley Girley pounded across the line, victorious.

The pandemonium was earsplitting, and although nobody but Jamie Freestone made any real money that day, it was a glorious win.

When the announcer officially called the race, thousands of race-goers littered the ground with betting slip confetti. And Shirley Girley cantered back to the winners circle to receive the cup.

• • •

Having picked their way to the Freestone box, Jamie introduced Bill and Emily to the assembled guests. And as Bill shook hands with an the impeccably dressed foreigner, sporting sun bleached hair, and the sort of tan you only get from spending time in the most exotic island hideaways, Emily's heart stopped.

She was face-to-face with Jack Clemmons.

Emily woodenly took Jack's hand. And in the split second their fingers touched, the electricity of desire surged from his hand to hers. She was instantly fearful Jack might inadvertently reveal their acquaintance and ruin everything with Bill. And all she could think of was, *of all days, in all places, why now?* With her emotions in total disarray, the blood drained from her face. And as dizziness overcame her, she grabbed Bill's arm.

"Em, darling, are you all right?" Bill asked. "Do you want to go back to—?"

"Bill," interrupted Jamie. "As you played such a huge part in my buying Shirley, you have to come meet the star of the show."

"I'm not sure I can, Jamie, Em doesn't look well. We better return to my box, I think the crush here is bothering her."

Jack stepped forward. "That would be such a shame, Bill. As I've met the beautiful creature in question…" He avoided looking in Emily's direction. "I'd be happy to escort Miss. Wilks and wait with her until you return."

Bill ran a hand down Emily's arm. "What do you think, darling, will you be all right with young Clemmons for a few minutes?"

With hands trembling, and heart pounding, Emily nodded an okay.

"Good, I'll be as quick as I can." Bill pecked her reassuringly on the cheek and pulled Jack aside. "I think you should take Emily's arm, she looks a bit wobbly. If she wants to lie down, speak to Jonesy, the steward. I don't know how long this will take but there are plenty of refreshments in my box; feel free to help yourself." He moved back to Emily. "Okay, darling, everything is set. Don't play the martyr, let Jack take a hold of your arm, and if you need to, lie down 'til I get back."

· · ·

The pair walked wordlessly towards Bill's box, and upon finding a secluded corner, Jack repositioned his arm around Emily's waist, and pulled her into his embrace. "My God, Emily, what happened in Monaco?" In the hubbub of the racetrack, his whisper was almost inaudible.

Emily buried her face into Jack's shoulder, and it was several seconds before she pulled herself together. "I'm so sorry. I had no choice but to leave. Jude got into some trouble, and when I challenged her, she attacked me."

"So she did put the bruises on your face."

"How do you know about that?"

Jack pushed her hair back. "When I asked The Hermitage for your address, the GSD remembered you, and said when you checked out, you looked beaten up."

"And you came looking for me?"

"To see if you were all right. I knew you wouldn't willingly leave without saying goodbye."

"If you knew my address, why didn't you contact me?"

"I couldn't."

"Your father?"

"No, the police. They told me what Jude was mixed up in, and by leaving Monaco with her, you were dragged into it. I was under orders to say nothing in case you warned her they were looking for her."

"I couldn't help it, Jack. She reminded me of how much she'd helped me after my parents and grandmother died. I tried to stand up to her, but she can be very violent. She intercepted a message I gave to the desk clerk, and threatened to kill me. I was afraid. She put me under pressure, and I caved. Then on the flight home, she told me about the fistfight with the woman who stole her money. She said she escaped when the woman fell onto a coffee table. We fled the hotel because the woman and an accomplice said they were coming after her."

Tears flowed down her cheeks and for the first time Jack realized behind Emily's confident and capable exterior there hid a frightened little girl. He wanted so much to protect her from the bad things that had happened.

"It's all over now," he whispered. "We'll contact the police, tell them everything and pick up where we left off. Jude and all her misery can go to hell."

Emily took a Kleenex from her purse, and dabbed her eyes. "Where we left off? Jack, there is no left off. We had one dinner together. Besides, as you so often said, it's not that easy."

"Of course it is, you're single, I'm single, what's not easy?"

"We had a wonderful few hours in Monaco. But I'm committed to Bill."

"Well I have to say it is a shock to know that the *gentleman* friend you talked about, is multi-millionaire Bill Bailey. The Bill Bailey who just asked me to guard you with my life."

Emily frowned. "Jack, seriously, whatever you wish between us is simply that. I belong to Bill. Everything you think I am is thanks to the peace of mind he gives me. And I'll never again do anything that might hurt him. You could be everything I dreamed about, but I can't be with you. You have to go away—right now—and forget me."

"First, let's straighten something out. I don't have money like Bill Bailey or my father, which makes us equal. *We* are on the same level. Ordinary, everyday working stiffs. Together, we can make a life. We don't have to be answerable to men who are used to buying everything and everybody."

"Answerable? I'm not answerable to Bill the way you are with your father. I don't know what impression I gave you, but I love Bill. Being with him is a pleasure, not a curse. I have a job and make my own money. I'm with him because it's where I want to be. You're bitter and hurt about your life, because you're stuck in a place you hate."

"Was," said Jack.

"Excuse me?"

"Was—Jaime talked me up to the Director of his brokerage house, and I start a new job in the city next week."

"That's good, Jack, you finally broke free from your father. And I finally broke free from Jude. But make no mistake, at some point in the not-too-distant future, Bill and I will be married."

Jack stepped back from Emily. "Oh, I'm sorry, I didn't mean to…I had no idea you and he were that serious. When we were together I thought we had…I'm sorry I did get the wrong impression. I assumed too much and wasn't thinking rationally. Please forgive me." Jack was devastated, but composed himself. "Did the police finally arrest her?"

"Arrest who?" asked Emily.

"Jude, because of Monaco; she beat that young woman and left her to bleed to death."

It was as if Jack had slapped her across the face. "What? Jude said they had a fight and she ran when the woman hit her head on a coffee table."

"My friend at police headquarters told me she did hit her head, but according to the coroner, Jude probably stood there a while, and then left her to bleed to death. There are pictures with footpri—"

"Oh God!" With a gasp of guilt and regret, Emily covered her face with her hands.

"Emily, what's happening? You didn't do anything."

"That's the whole point. I didn't *do* anything. Jude beat that woman, then me. If I'd been stronger, called the police, I might have saved that woman's life. God, I am such a coward, I never *do* anything."

"You're not making sense; you didn't know Jude was lying."

"But I did. She's always lying; making up stories, cheating people and blaming others. Every bad decision she ever made is because of what someone else did. It's been like that ever since I've known her. And God help me, this isn't the first incident."

"She's killed someone else?"

Emily nodded. "I can't prove it, but I'm sure of it."

"Jesus Christ, you have to tell me what the hell is going on here."

"Years ago, Jude and I went up to Bear Mountain and met up with a young couple. We drank a lot and after I left Jude with them, there was a car accident. The two kids, along with two others travelling in the opposite direction, died in a head-on crash. I wasn't there, but when I learned about the circumstances and location of the accident, and recalled the state Jude was in the next day, I knew she was involved. But, I didn't do anything."

"That wasn't your—"

"There's more. Later Tina, Jude's companion, told me she owed some friends money in Jackson Heights. I loaned her a couple of hundred dollars, although my heart knew she would probably use it to buy drugs. She was killed in a hit-and-run that the police declared was related to a drug deal gone bad. I could have refused to give her money, stopped her from going. Jesus, if I'd have told the police what was happening, she might still be alive. But I didn't *do* anything."

"Emily, none of this is—"

Emily put up a hand to quiet Jack. "Not long ago, I had a suspicion, things—bad things—were being smuggled through the airport. I watched for a while and certain restricted items that were supposed to go to customs would simply vanish with no paper trail, no receipts, and no bills of lading. Because she's on the opposite shift to me, I tentatively approached Jude and asked her if she had noticed anything weird, and she said I was imagining things. I checked the files, Jack, double-and triple-checked every item. All the missing stuff arrived late at night on my shift and was gone the next day before anyone else on Jude's shift saw it. But, once again, once a pathetic thing again, I…did…not…*do*…anything. I'm a pitiful excuse for a female with zip in the way of integrity."

Jack took her hand in his. "I'm no shrink, but I've indulged in enough sob sessions to know you've spent years forgiving the wrong people for bad things. In the process, you've loaded yourself down with such guilt it's going to take more than a hug and a Band-Aid to get you out. But we can fix this."

"And precisely how do I convince the police that I was beaten and kidnapped by my roommate, but 'til today, I still lived with her. And oops, sorry, I forgot to mention years ago she got two kids drunk and might be responsible for their deaths, and two others, on Bear Mountain. And there's more. A few weeks ago, I know she got into a bloody altercation with a woman in Monaco, who subsequently died. And if all that wasn't bad enough, right now, as we speak, she is probably smuggling God knows what all else in and out of JFK!"

"All I heard is, you suspect a lot of things, but have proof of nothing. Your only crime is not telling the authorities what you suspect. Let me talk to my father's lawyers, they sorted my mess out, and know how to spin things in a positive direction."

"A positive direction? My God, is that the mother of all understatements or what? My conscience needs more than a lawyer's quick fix. I have to face down my demons, and I'm doing that by quitting my job at Transcontinental, and leaving New York. I'm putting as much distance as I can between Jude and me by moving in with Bill. And under no circumstances do I want you any more involved than you are."

Before Jack could protest, Bill was beside them.

"Good grief, Em," Bill said. "What happened? You look terrible." He felt her forehead. "You're burning up. We should get you to a doctor."

She hated to lie to him, but in the circumstances, she felt it necessary. "I'm okay, Bill. Jack just told me a mutual acquaintance was murdered."

"I'm so sorry, darling, that's an awful thing to hear. Let's scoot on home; familiar surroundings are always best when dealing with bad news." He reached out to shake Jack's hand. "Thanks so much for keeping an eye on things. I know you're bunking at Jamie's right now, but you're very welcome to stay at Harrington Hall if you need a change of venue. What say you, Em?"

Emily smiled thinly.

"That's very nice of you both," said Jack woodenly. "Might I take a rain check? I have business in the city that requires my full attention."

Chapter Eleven

Emily watched the trees stream by. No words accompanied their journey and her tears fell with each passing mile. However, as the roof of Harrington Hall loomed large, she dabbed her eyes, took a stabilizing breath and squeezed Bill's hand. "I'm sorry to be such a baby."

"It's a shock to hear something like that. I don't think I've ever seen you so upset about anything. Are you really all right?"

"Nothing that one of Brothers special pick-me-ups can't cure."

"There's my stoic gal. Nothing keeps you down for long."

· · ·

Brothers had set up cocktails in the conservatory, and Bill handed one to Emily.

"This was a good suggestion," she said, after taking a sip. "And I have another."

Bill raised an eyebrow and leered theatrically. "Oh yes, my pretty?"

"Not that, you rogue. I want to go back to New York and collect my things immediately."

"The gang will be expecting you at dinner. Can't it wait until tomorrow?"

She put down her drink. "No. My decision to move here is made. I'm eager to tie up some loose ends, and start our new life."

"Give me a list, I'll call the office and have someone do all that."

Emily came alongside, and wrapped her arms about him. "This is something I have to do Bill. I want to clean out my apartment, and give notice at Transcontinental."

"Leave the apartment, there's nothing you need. And write a note for Transcon'. Joe can deliver it and tell whomever to deal with it. I don't want you to leave me."

The uncharacteristic hardness of his attitude made her giggle. "I'm not leaving you, silly, I'll be right back. I'll do the note to Transcontinental, because I really don't want to risk running in to Jude. But I'm stripping that apartment of everything you ever gave me."

"I can buy more. I'm rich, remember?"

"I really have to do this, darling. Joe can fly me to JFK, stay at The Pierre overnight, then at first light pick me up, and bring me back. Eighteen hours tops and I'll be on the lawn…okay?"

It didn't happen often but Bill knew when he was beaten. "I miss you already."

•••

The dogs howled mournfully as the rotor whine increased and their mistress was elevated into the chill evening air. Watching Bill far below, she had never seen him look so vulnerable, and when a fleeting memory of her parents leaving her at her grandmother's house caused her to shudder, she almost had Joe turn back.

Chapter Twelve

An airline warehouse at JFK, or any other airport for that matter, has no redeeming features. They are noisy, dirty, and soulless, and the only reason most people work in them is because the job generally pays well, and usually has a decent medical plan. In addition, the airline allows its employees to break out of the box by travelling the world at a discounted rate, and Jude Cameron had been reaping one other benefit for some years. She'd earned gambling money 'rerouting' certain merchandise away from the watchful eye of the U.S. Customs service. And her accomplice in expeditiously removing many of the re-routed items was T.W. Ford, the pilot owner of SkoogAir, a small cargo carrier based in Sanford, Maine.

• • •

Jude walked into work with a 'kiss my ass' attitude. Her life had finally turned around, and by noon she'd be halfway to an exotic island, with a quarter million bucks in an off-shore bank account.

It didn't take long for the warehouse team to notice how happy she was, and she endured the usual teasing about finally making it with this or that woman she'd talked about. However, despite busting to tell them all to shove their condescending innuendo up their asses, she ignored them and proceeded with her routine.

Being the senior agent, Jude strode about the warehouse checking the export containers loads. Satisfied that nothing was amiss which might prompt someone to distract her from her mission, she reviewed paperwork on imports. She had always paid particular attention to incoming valuables, fantasizing what it might be like to have just a tiny piece of the pie, and now, as she struggled to contain her excitement, she noted the arrival of an additional and very large diamond shipment.

Jude took a deep breath as she stole a glance about, then with shaking hands, she walked to the warehouse phone, dialed the cell number she'd been given, and said, "are we playing ball today?" The monotone voice at the end of the line answered "yes" and the game was on.

Concentrating on any sort of work after that became difficult, and every time the office door opened, Jude hoped it wasn't the Customs appraiser's team arriving early. Interrogating the clock as it inexorably ticked toward ten; Jude downed three cups of coffee, and practically asphyxiated the warehouse's bats as she burned through a pack of Marlboros. But the cigarettes did little to calm her nerves, and the excess of coffee had her guts turning cartwheels. She decided that filing might keep her grounded.

When next she looked at the clock, it was after ten, and with sweat beading on her lip, Jude trawled her desk drawer for more cigarettes. She was startled when Lou, from the Customs appraiser's office burst in.

"Goddamn big-dig pain in the ass, waste of tax-paper money. Hi Jude, how's it hanging?"

Jude spun around. "Lou, er, hi. It's not like you to be late."

"Goddamn traffic was bumper-to-bumper, and now it's ten after. I swear if I ever get hold of the numb-nuts moron who started that project, I'll nail his ass to the wall."

Jude smiled nervously. "Tell it like it is, Lou."

"Sorry, but a man can't even go about his business anymore."

"You're just ten minutes off schedule. No big deal, you still got time to sit. I bought in some Dunkin for you."

Lou opened the box and pulled out a doughnut. "Now that's real nice, Jude, you know how I love my apple crumb."

"Frank not with you today?"

"Yea, he's outside. Kid from Continental brought that Hummer over for him to see."

"I heard about that. Where's a cargo-chucker getting the money for a Hummer?"

Lou took a bite of the cake. "Man these are good. Foxboro; he won a hundred grand on one friggin spin of the wheel."

"Lucky stiff, I never win squat."

"Amen sister, I hear you. Here, this is today's list. Can I have another bun?"

"Sure. Eight tins?" asked Jude.

"Yeah there's some sort of diamond cutters expo at the arena. Between you and me, this amount of ice will be coming in for a while."

In the wake of Lou's whirlwind arrival, Frank lumbered in. "Jeez Louise, that piece of shit kid can't be more 'an twenty and he's already got his...hey Jude, you got any crullers in that box?"

"Sure do, help yourself, and I just made a pot."

"I always love coming to Transcon'. Don't I say that, Lou? You guys are so civilized. Get jack anywhere else. Hey Lou, go light on the half-and-half, what am I, calcium-deficient?"

"You got some sort of deficient, now stop belly-aching. I swear if you don't got anything to bitch about, you'd bitch about that."

Jude smiled at her friends' bickering. "Okay guys, before World War three breaks out, I'm gone. Be right back, now eat your cake and play nice."

As the guys hoisted their doughnuts aloft, Jude headed into the warehouse. Blood pounded so loudly in her temples, she felt sure they'd hear it. So she took a deep breath, and made the walk she'd completed a thousand times. Today, however, she had exactly the right incentive to do what everyone knew in theory could be done, but never for one minute, thought they could get away with.

Setting off at a good clip, Jude couldn't help thinking about the job's simplicity, and knowing that Lou Willis and Frank Mason were the armed guards waiting in reception, her confidence in the mission's outcome soared.

She'd known Lou and Frank for years. They were great guys, each on the wrong side of fifty, with personality to spare. But Jude knew, with absolute certainty, whenever they turned up at Transcontinental; they never spent less than an hour bull-shitting in reception. That downtime was critical for the plan to work, and from the minute she left the import office with their gem list, it would be at least an hour before either man stopped talking long enough to realize their shipment hadn't been delivered to them. By that time, with T.W.'s Bonanza at full throttle, she would be on her way to paradise, and a life she'd only dreamed about.

As Jude disappeared into the import area, she glanced at her watch, 10:17 A.M. She'd covered the hundred or so yards quickly, knowing every minute was critical, and as she turned to pass the ramp doorway, she was delighted to see T.W.'s Bonanza parked outside. She could also see the refueling truck attached, and as she approached the safe area, the familiar figure of T.W., wearing his signature Australian bush hat, sauntered toward the checkout desk. Without acknowledging her accomplice, Jude walked on, called the Duty Officer down from his second floor office, and made her way to the vault to meet him.

T.W. heard the D.O. clomping down the stairs, but never raised his head. He simply dropped off his articles for export, and inquired if he had any packages for the onward leg to Philly. When he received an answer in the negative, he picked up his papers, and sauntered back to his aircraft. 10:19 A.M.

As the refueling truck was unhooking T.W's Bonanza, he knew Jude had tied up with the D.O. at the vault. He signed his credit card receipt, boarded his aircraft and prepared to get under way. 10:22 A.M.

At the vault, the D.O. flipped the tumbler, and having set a combination Jude knew had been the same for several years, he inserted his key, turned it twice, and swung open the bulky door. Jude knew the vault well. It had walls of metal racks that held dozens of eight-by-five gem tins, an assortment of aircraft parts, electronic equipment, and other valuable cargo. Without hesitation, she stepped into the pitch darkness, took a step right and flipped the light switch. The naked bulb flooded the space with its cold, hard brilliance, and though she'd never felt claustrophobic before, today, her breath came in short sharp bursts. For an instant, she felt as if the walls were closing about her, telling her to get out while she could. But she knew it was just the enormity of what she was doing. And as she turned back to the open door, and saw the D.O. holding it ajar, she was able to divert her panic to another place.

Consulting the customs clipboard, eight tins were listed for collection. The first six were Walvis Bay Holdings...*good*, she thought, *all together in the same place*. She pulled them quickly, and memorizing the final two label numbers, methodically scanned the racks. Then, having pulled all eight tins, Jude stacked the cloth wrapped bundles on the collapsible worktop affixed to the vault door.

The D.O. took her clipboard, adjusted the vault inventory log, and placed the shipment back into Jude's waiting arms. The entire shipment weighed less than three pounds. 10:27 A.M.

Biting her lip and focusing on walking, Jude managed to control herself well enough. However, when she came to the door connecting export and import warehouses she started to shake And, as she glanced out to the tarmac, and saw the Bonanza slowly creeping toward her, the split-second of distraction, had her catching the clipboard on the door jamb. A gem tin thudded to the floor. "Shit a brick," she mumbled.

"Yo, Jude," shouted the D.O., about to ascend to his office. "You need some help in there?"

"Sorry, boss; dropped a tin is all."

"Long as you don't spill ice all over the damn floor. Feds don't like that sort of clean–up."

"I got it. Thanks anyway. That your phone ringing?"

"Jeez, I've got a ten-thirty conference with marketing, sure you can manage?"

Stooping awkwardly to pick up the tin, Jude waved. "Yeah go, you know how bent sales gets if we don't dance to their tune."

"Ain't that the truth," answered the D.O., scurrying up the stairs.

Jude took a minute to compose herself, then looking around and finding no one in her part of the warehouse, she ducked out to her right. A short jog across the ramp had her alongside the Bonanza, which had rolled into the blind spot between import and export warehouses. Jude quickened her pace to line up with the aircraft's open door. Then with her final stride, she threw the tins inside, jumped into the airplane, and pulled the door shut behind her.

When T.W. felt the jolt of Jude hitting the fuselage floor, he opened the throttle. And before the Bonanza's door was fully locked and secure, he rolled from the cargo ramp onto the taxiway. 10:30 A.M.

Continuing his tower-speak as if he were on his routine flight plan to Philadelphia, T.W. knew his taxi-time to the take-off runway could take twenty minutes. That was five more minutes than this operation could afford. So, hitting the gas, he sped to the runway, and made up the time lost by the late customs drivers. The Bonanza came to a rocking halt and settled in line. 10:43 A.M.

With SkoogAir cargo to Philadelphia now right on schedule, and impatiently positioned for departure, T.W. checked the aircraft line up. It looked like there was some congestion up front with the wide bodies, and he cursed. Waiting for takeoff behind a bunch of lumbering behemoths was irritating and time consuming at any time, but today an uncharacteristic bead of sweat ran down his temple. He wasn't nervous about being the little guy behind such powerful jets. His only concern was getting far away from JFK before the customs team realized they'd not received their tins. At that point, Jude would also be missed, someone would hit the panic button, and all hell would break loose. The pilot re-contacted the tower about his wait time, and was instructed to hold. 10:45 A.M.

Three long minutes later, as aircraft appeared to be moving T.W. noted the two wide bodies ahead of him. His mind was in overdrive as he watched the Air India 747 roll down the runway. His fingers fanned the controls, tapping out a nervous tattoo. "Go baby go," he mumbled to nobody in particular. "Get out of papa's way." 10:50 A.M.

Tickling the controls to push a little further forward, T.W. knew he'd be cutting it fine to pull off this particular stunt. But he'd been in tight spots before, and adrenaline took over. With one ahead, and less than ten minutes to meltdown, he focused on the tower cross talk. *"Airbus 180, you are clear to taxi, line up on runway…"*

T.W.'s grip on the stick tightened as the Air France Airbus sat "Shit man," he screamed into the ether. "What the hell are you waiting for? Wind the sum bitch up why don't ya." 10:53 A.M.

As the Airbus sat, T.W.'s nerves started to fray. "Shit, shit, shit!" he yelled, slapping the consol. "Move it, you cretin." The Airbus moved nowhere. And as the early morning sun streamed through the Bonanza's huge window, sweat ran down his neck. "Okay, okay," T.W. mumbled to himself. "Hold it together, we've been in tighter spots than this, it'll move, give it a minute…A MINUTE I DON'T FUCKING HAVE…" As he screamed the last, hoping to push the Air France Airbus forward, a voice echoed in his headset.

"SkoogAir light, this is the tower."

Deep breathing pulled him back to pilot calm, and without a trace of tension in his voice T.W. responded. "SkoogAir 3649, tower, go ahead." 10:55 A.M.

"SkoogAir 3649, get ready to roll Captain, the Airbus ahead is having brake problems. We need to keep this show on the road, so line up on runway 24."

"SkoogAir 3649, copy, runway 24." 10:56 A.M.

T.W. smiled as the Bonanza rolled to its takeoff position on the runway, and with engines throbbing, waited for word from the tower. "Come on, son, say the word…just say it, and let old Uncle Skoog out of here, before he pisses his pants." 10:58 A.M.

The Bonanza sat and rocked.

"Come on people, I'm still waiting…got places to go, people to see." 10.59 A.M.

When word came, it resonated inordinately loud.

"SkoogAir 3649, clear for takeoff, have a good day Captain."

"SkoogAir 3649, thank you tower." As the engine raced and the Bonanza rolled forward, T.W. beamed. 11:04 A.M.

"Move, baby move," he yelled to his airplane. "Give me power baby, more power…" As the wheels lifted from the ground and the tarmac flashed beneath, T.W. let out a whoop. "Yee-ha! We have lift-off. Let's suck up the gear, get the hell out of here. Elvis has left the building."

T.W. had one ear listening, should there be contrary instructions, but no matter what, in his mind, he was gone. And as he looked back to see Jude laying prostrate on the cabin floor, the Bonanza climbed effortlessly into a cloudless blue sky, heading for the City of Brotherly Love.

Chapter Thirteen

Customs office courier Lou was in fine form, declaring that after six months of purgatory, interspersed with dubious boosts from 'the patch,' he'd finally given up smoking. Frank more quietly touted his knowledge of all things football, declaring that with the aid of the Packers, Patriots, Ravens, Broncos and Falcons, he'd won five thousand dollars in the office pool. And as the Transcontinental cargo team gathered in reception, pretty much everyone had an opinion on where it could best be spent. Frank quietly smiled, for had they known about his penchant for gambling, they'd understand why the money was long gone back into his bookie's bottomless pocket.

Also long gone—SkoogAir.

It was 11:07 A.M. when the Duty Officer joined the gabfest and Lou noticed he wasn't carrying their gem tins. "Yo Mack, we gotta problem?"

The D.O. flipped the empty Dunkin box. "Yeah we got a problem, you greedy sons of monkeys ate all the donuts."

"Not what I had in mind," said Lou. "You still see Frank and me here, right."

The D.O. nodded. "So?"

"So we don't got our friggin' tins."

The blank look on the D.O.'s face spoke volumes. "I gave them to Jude," he said consulting his watch. "Forty minutes ago."

Lou looked at Frank. "She didn't come this way, so where's my tins?"

"There's no other way out, except—" The D.O. turned toward the tarmac. "Oh, crap!"

"Holy Mother of God," said Lou. "Frank, get to the van and hit the panic button."

Then the shit hit the fan.

11:10 A.M.

Chapter Fourteen

T.W. smiled broadly as the Bonanza droned on. It was the smile of a man who'd spent twenty years of slogging his guts out for pennies and was finally about to make the dollars he'd always expected. His SkoogAir service came down from Portland to JFK every morning and whether or not he picked up more cargo, his flight plan took him on to Philadelphia, Baltimore and Washington. Today, however, after take-off from JFK, he would make his pass over the Teterboro beacon in New Jersey, and begin his flight to Paradise.

"You strapped in?" he called to Jude.

"Yeah why, are we going through turbulence?"

"You better believe it." T.W. was at the beacon when he squawked a 'mayday'. Then he put the Bonanza's nose down, dropped his wing, and rolled the aircraft into a spiral dive. "Hang on," he yelled. "We're going down."

"What the fuck!" screamed Jude.

Poor cow, T.W. thought. *She doesn't know the half of what's to come.* And as he calmly watched the altimeter spin down toward five hundred feet, he flipped off the transponder.

With the fear of God in her, Jude wedged her knees tight against the seat in front of her. For a scant moment, she prayed to any gods that would listen, promising eternal devotion should they deliver her from the mess in which she found herself. But as terror froze her body in a numbing paralysis, her mind was surprisingly clear. She knew the Bonanza didn't fly as high as a commercial jet, and they'd hit the ground quickly. She put a death grip on the armrests, closed her eyes, and counted down to impact.

As she mouthed 'zero' she was thrown back into her seat with such pressure she thought her back would break. Then she felt the aircraft level off.

Jude slowly opened one eye, patted the seat in front, and looked down at her wiggling feet. Then, she laughed. She was still thinking, breathing and sweating. T.W. had done it. The old buzzard had pulled them from the brink. She unfolded herself from the position in which she'd braced, rubbed her arms and legs to restore the circulation, and leaned toward the window. A blinding flash accompanied the aircraft breaking land, and now it appeared they were flying at a frighteningly low altitude, over the ocean.

Jude's sense of relief was short-lived. She'd never liked flying in small aircraft, and since she'd been involved in a near drowning incident as a child, liked the ocean even less. Now the combination of a small aircraft flying low over the ocean, rekindled fears she thought were under control.

T.W. looked straight ahead at the vast expanse of ocean he had to navigate, and flipped the switch to integrate the auxiliary fuel tanks. Then, cranking up the power, he headed on a direct course to Bermuda. Having used low-level flight to transport dubious commodities of particularly high value, in the past, T.W. knew the authorities couldn't see him on their radar. And after his mayday, with no transponder active, their natural assumption would be that he'd crashed shortly after crossing the Teterboro beacon. With luck, by the time they made a cursory examination of the area and determined he'd not succumbed to an untimely demise, the Bonanza would be well on its way to the rendezvous point. There he'd hand over the gem tins, and be transported to the Bahamian Island of Great Abaco, along with his second million dollars.

...

Flying over a seemingly endless expanse of open water made Jude nervous, and after what felt like several hours, she still didn't know where they were going. Moving forward, she entered the cockpit, where the large front windows displayed water, for more miles than she cared to see. T.W. was engrossed in his instruments, and Jude was not sure whether she should disturb him. However, feeling it was about time she knew what was going on, she tapped him on the shoulder. Her surprise approach caused him to jump half out of his seat, and feeling mildly vindicated that he had in some small way received the same kind of shock he'd given her, Jude smiled.

"So where are we going?" she yelled above the engine noise.

"Doesn't really matter for you."

"Excuse me?" she said, leaning forward to hear him better.

Smiling pleasantly, T.W. pulled a pistol from his seat pocket, twisted in his seat, and shot her once in the chest.

Jude's body recoiled back into the cabin, oozing dark red blood, and as she focused on the blood—her blood—she felt remarkably calm. The droning whine of the Bonanza's engines sounded like a bizarre heavenly chorus. It brought her a strange kind of peace; until all the bad things from her life flashed vividly in her mind.

...

After pocketing his gun, T.W. nonchalantly returned to his instruments, and it was some time before he spotted a large sport-fishing vessel ahead, silver white and painfully small on the vast expanse of blue. As he drew closer, the tiny metal island, with purple upper decks and familiar company helicopter, was the haven he'd been looking for.

Buzzing the vessel, he tipped the Bonanza's wings and 'yee-ha-ed' silently as a guy with a flare gun waved. T.W. flew on and then came about in a wide circle, waiting for the recognition signal.

When a bright light flashed by him and exploded into a million dollars of happy lights, he smiled, re-set his instruments, and engaged the Bonanza's autopilot.

T.W. had practiced in the local pool, as it had been many years since his Pensacola training had him bailing out of an aircraft into an actual ocean. But, as he knew from experience, fear and doubt were the jumper killers. The major key to parachuting into the ocean was mental preparation. And he was one hundred percent ready to glide into the ocean with the gem tins, and tread water until he was picked up. He was doubly confident of his success, knowing that unlike his last testosterone-fueled Marine equipped jump, today he'd be wearing a specially constructed life jacket, and an H2O parachute designed by BASE jumpers for water landings.

Hurrying to the aft locker, where the gear was stowed, T.W.'s practiced hands secured the straps on the bulky life jacket. Then, he cinched himself loosely into the chute, leaving room to secure the gem tins in the jacket's pockets. To his annoyance, when he made his way back to the area in which Jude had been sitting, the gem tins were gone. Assuming the aircraft's sharp descent had caused them to slide to the front of the cabin, he moved forward. He cursed upon discovering that when he'd shot Jude, she'd fallen onto some of the unrestrained tins. Now he had to waste time wrestling her out of the way.

Bending to shift her considerable bulk, T.W. wondered how much more aggravation he'd have to take. Then a vision of Great Abaco's golden beaches put everything into perspective. A broad smile crept across his face as he shoved Jude roughly aside. And while his life jacket had six pockets to accommodate the expected number of gem tins, there, as if an apology for the inconveniences he'd suffered, lay eight. The unexpected bonus was just what was needed to spur him on, and breaking open two of the tins; he poured the contents into his flight suit's zippered pockets. He then loaded the remaining tins into the life jacket's pockets and cinched his parachute tight. Feeling like an ad for Michelin tires, he turned back to the aircraft's controls.

Sweat streamed down T.W.'s face as he perched astride his seat and made adjustments to climb high enough for his jump into the recovery area around the fishing vessel. And after waiting a few seconds for the instruments to kick in, he waddled into the cabin, to pop the rear door.

By the time he saw Jude's hand, wielding a box-cutter, it was too late.

T.W. watched helplessly as blood seeped through the fabric of his flight suit. Had the cut been direct to his groin, he knew he'd have bled to death in seconds. As it was, Jude had connected with one of his diamond-filled thigh pockets. Now part of his secret stash rained down upon her.

"Fucking bitch!" he spat, looking down into Jude's glassy albeit defiant eyes. "Now you've really pissed me off."

Clutching at the growing patch of red, T.W. vigorously attempted to free his leg from Jude's grasp. But she had a death grip on his pants leg. He attempted to haul her across the cabin. Her grip held fast. He wrestled the dead weight of her body as best he could, until he feared the autopilot might disengage. Then he braced his upper body against the seats, and kicked her full force in the head. He watched in silence as his diamonds turned to rubies in a bloody pool on the floor.

Jude let out an ominous throat rattle and her hand dropped.

Dragging his bleeding leg across her, T.W. limped to the first aid kit. He was searching for something to make a tourniquet, as the last thing he wanted was to have a bloody leg dangling in open water. After frantically emptying the emergency locker, he couldn't find what he needed. He improvised using a cargo line. Cursing like a longshoreman, he lashed the rope tightly around his thigh, and the bleeding stopped. Then, after dousing his leg with the emergency locker's iodine, he limped to the door.

As T.W. put his fist through the "emergency open" casing, a piercing shriek assaulted his ears. He snapped down the lever, and anxiously waited as the explosive release engaged, to propel the detached door backwards. And as he watched the door spiral into oblivion, he looked down. He could no longer see the fishing vessel beneath. The delaying tussle with Jude had clearly taken him beyond the rendezvous circle. But there was no time for adjustments. As the wind-rush froze his face, and a Hail Mary escaped his lips, the wounded pilot launched himself into space and tumbled after the door.

The first few seconds of airtime were more than normally disorienting. However, as he told himself that loss of blood was the cause, he cleared the aircraft slipstream and positioned for free fall. Frigid air buffeted his spread-eagle descent, painfully chafing his flight suit against his leg's open wound. Nevertheless, he gritted his teeth and focused on his impending reward.

When his chute opened at seven-hundred-and-fifty feet, he looked down and saw the extreme cold of altitude had conveniently fused the flight-suit fabric to his leg. And as he floated silently down, T.W. smiled. *There is a God after all.*

Looking back at his beloved Bonanza on a heading for a watery grave; a pang of regret bit deep. The old gal had been a good and faithful companion, and he would miss her. But before any tears were shed for his old friend, he saw the fishing vessel streaming fast to his position.

With a bum leg, T.W. knew a heavy impact on the water might do some serious damage. So reviewing the landing routine in his mind, he decided to lean back a few degrees before touchdown, and apply the brakes a few feet above water. He'd release his chute away from his body before it dragged him about, and as the life jacket automatically activated on contact with water; there was no chance he would sink.

The water approached faster than T.W. remembered giving him a niggling doubt about his abilities. Then he reminded himself that in his youth, he was an accomplished parachutist. Jumping was just like riding a bike; you never forget. He continued to shake, because while it was true he'd completed hundreds of jumps over land, he couldn't deny, his dozen or so jumps into the ocean had bothered him.

As the pilot fought to keep his nerves in check, he attempted to maneuver his H2O closer to the oncoming vessel, and in doing so experienced a snag in one of the risers. He countered using delicate persuasion, and got it to cooperate, but rather than risk additional drift away from the oncoming vessel he made a large circle to its rear. If necessary, he wanted to establish a swimming distance he thought manageable. As T.W. counted down, he leaned back, applied the brakes a couple of feet above the waves, and snapped the H2O's release. The chute careened behind him on the stiffening ocean breeze.

The pilot hit the water bottom heavy. But as soon as the jacket touched water, it burst to life and buoyed him high. Thanking his own version of God, T.W. spread his arms and waited for his rescuers.

Bobbing powerless in the growing waves, T.W. couldn't stop focusing on the amount of time the boat was taking to get to him. It seemed a lot longer than he'd anticipated, although a glance at his watch told him it was only eight minutes. So, beginning with 'Mary had a little lamb,' he diverted his mind from the increasing dread he felt. For a while, the simple rhyme calmed him, nevertheless, his thoughts kept returning to the last time he was in a rolling ocean. He was much younger then, with rescuers closer, in a controlled jump, and he didn't have a shark-bait leg to ponder.

Looking again at his watch, twelve minutes had passed. And as salt water mingled with the sweat pouring from his body, he knew only one thing prompted real fear in those adrift on the ocean. For him, now, it wasn't the water. He had a good life jacket, which boosted him high atop the growing swell. He was perfectly safe. It wasn't being alone; he was in his rescuer's sights. They were heading directly for him. It wasn't his leg. It had become numb, and with no way to ease the tourniquet, he may already have done more damage than he anticipated. That was fixable. It was the specter of a predator.

Deep cerebral fear poured from him, and ignoring his injury, T.W. kicked his legs as hard as he could in an attempt to swim to the oncoming vessel. He tried but failed. The jacket held him fast. He simply succeeded in lifting himself higher atop the waves. But just as his fear morphed to panic, he saw his rescuers but yards away. Flooded with relief, T.W. churned out 'Mary had a little lamb' again, and resigned himself to a few seconds of patience.

Then he felt a jolt.

Like someone had run into him with a shopping cart.

It didn't hurt.

But it was freaking annoying.

Then he saw blood.

Lots of blood.

T.W. knew that the merciless denizens of the deep smelled blood from miles away, and could move faster below the water than most anything above. He had to do something to help himself. Cursing himself for not checking his makeshift tourniquet, he reached down. There was nothing there. Not just the rope, there was nothing. No leg, nothing. And the primeval dread he previously felt exploded into a frenzy of terror. He had to move. Get away. He frantically flailed, and only succeeded in further spreading his blood. He thrashed at the waves. But his super-inflated jacket rendered him armless.

Then the shopping cart hit again.

This time, the warm feeling permeating T.W.'s body caused an inner calm he'd never felt before. When the third hit came, the ocean ran crimson, and he couldn't understand why he was still alive. Feeling no pain, and remarkably at peace, his mind drifted to a happier place, and as he waited for the inevitable blackness, something tugged at his jacket. Opening is eyes, he could see the rescue pole attached to his shoulder strap, and thinking he'd dozed off amid some horrific dream, he reached for the gloved hand above him.

As hand grabbed fingers, and fingers met wrist, T.W. smiled. But the face of the man above was grim. And in the reflection of his sunglasses, T.W. saw the huge Mako shark leap out of the water.

Chapter Fifteen

When the phone rang, Emily expected it was Joe, saying he was delayed in rush hour traffic.

"Good morning, Miss Emily," said Bothers, a haunted quality in his voice.

"Brothers, hi, what's up?"

A palpable silence followed. "Miss Emily, I'm sorry to call you so early, did Joe arrive yet?"

"No, I thought you were him, he, it…you know what I mean. You don't sound right, old friend, what's going on?"

"Er, yes—I know what you mean. And, er, you are correct, things are most definitely not right. Miss Emily, I am so sorry, but I have some dreadful news."

Emily could imagine only one piece of news that would render the capable and businesslike Brothers, at a loss for words. "Has something happened to Bill?"

"Yes, miss, I was hoping Joe would be there by now. I didn't want you to be alone."

"Be alone? What happened?"

"It is my sad duty to inform you, Mr. Bailey has suffered a massive heart attack."

"Where is he," said Emily, blind-sided but remarkably calm. "Joe can take me directly there."

"Er…no, Miss…he's gone."

"Gone…gone where?" In her heart she knew, and prepared for her world to come crashing down.

"Miss Emily we are all so very sorry. Mr. Bailey died at 4:12 A.M."

Emily dropped the receiver and slumped in a chair. She heard Brothers shouting to pick up the phone, but all she wanted was to be left alone. Mind numb, and struggling to comprehend what had happened, she became aware of a knocking on the door. She opened it to find Joe.

When Joe enfolded her protectively in his arms, she couldn't hold back tears. He was saying something, and she knew she was supposed to go somewhere with him, but she couldn't get her thoughts in order. Her mind flew back to the night her grandmother said her parents were dead. She felt the same void, the mind numbing disbelief, and this time it was Bill. She had lost another piece of herself.

As Joe stroked her hair, Emily could hear the steady beating of his heart, and his words, whatever they were, calmed her. She let him lead her to a chair, and staring blankly through tears, her heart was brutalized by the finality of it all. She was in a state of paralysis as she watched Joe gather what she'd packed. She could see him coming and going, but it didn't register what he was doing. She could hear him speak; though his words made no sense. And when he lifted her from the chair, and said he was taking her home, she dropped her head on his shoulder, and let him carry her out.

Chapter Sixteen

When the helicopter touched down, Brothers was waiting, and Emily was considerably comforted to see him standing sentinel, as he always did. Joe set the helicopter to idle, reached for her hand, and squeezed it reassuringly. As he mouthed "okay?" she took a deep breath and nodded.

Even the dogs seemed subdued as Emily stepped onto the manicured lawn. They ran forward, she bent to pet them, and doled out cookies as she always did. But they left them untouched and followed her to the house.

As she slowly ascended the steps, she paused as if experiencing difficulty, but she was simply composing herself to face the inevitable emptiness of a home without Bill. Noticing her falter, Brothers stepped forward, and in an expression of familiarity rarely exhibited, encircled her with a supporting arm. He helped her into the house, but once across the threshold, returned to his circumspect self, asking her if there was anything he could get her. She said no, and proceeded to Bill's study.

$\bullet \bullet \bullet$

Entering Bill's sanctuary, Emily shivered. Everything was exactly as she remembered, walls lined with rare books, and cases filled with travel mementos. But it was palpably cold without his presence. Approaching the *Ekornes* recliner he used as an office chair, Emily half expected it to spin around, and reveal Bill sitting there. And as she ran her fingertips over the grain of the butter-soft leather, she remembered how he joked that the chair was smoother than his hide. Bittersweet memories cut deep into her heart, brutally highlighting the fact that she would never again hear his joking aggrandizement, witness his keen wit, or run her hands over his rugged body.

Glancing around, Emily was drawn to his desk and the glass-domed silver server that was so out of place. Bill had insisted it remain front and center as it contained little personal items she'd given him over the years. A sand dollar from Fiji where they first met, and a small tablet of soap from The Pierre. Decorative stones, an antique apothecary bottle, and a champagne cork. A piece of brain coral and a small swan made of aluminum foil. And though she could barely remember where some of the things came from, or why he'd kept them, they obviously marked an important milestone in their relationship.

Feeling a desperate need to connect, Emily sat in the recliner and closed her eyes. She sunk deep into the well-worn leather, and was so enveloped by the contours left by his body she almost felt he was holding her. And as she rested her head on the leather, she could smell his cologne. Tears flowed, for she knew, this was as close as she would ever be to him again.

When Brothers entered the study and coughed discreetly, he placed a tray with coffee and Mrs. Hudson's homemade shortbread, next to her. "Miss Emily," he said tenderly. "Mr. Bailey instructed me to tell you that when this happens, he has left an envelope for you in the drawer. I will leave you now, but you should look at it immediately."

Emily had never ventured into the desk's dark mahogany depths before, so she was surprised at the amount of effort needed on the antique brass drawer pull. And there, as if to accentuate the gravity of the moment was a lone envelope. She removed it, unwound the toggle fastener, and emptied the contents onto the desk. Her eyes immediately settled on a letter written in Bill's flowing hand. There was also a legal size portfolio, and a flat velvet box. She picked up the letter, and read the words Bill had written.

"My Dearest, most beloved Em:

How can I begin to tell you how happy you've made these last three years? From the minute we met, you made me feel young and alive, and it was only the frailty of this stupid body that prevented us from enjoying five—or maybe ten—more years. Don't be sad for me, darling. I had a good run, achieving almost everything I set out to do, and was surrounded by the most loving bunch of people imaginable.

Just to reassure you, our occasional gymnastics—which I wouldn't have traded for the world—had nothing to do with my heart giving out. I've known about my condition for quite some time, and did my very best to get plenty of rest. Ask Brothers, he'll tell you when you weren't here I spent an inordinate amount of time lolling about. Anyway, the last time we were together, and you made me as happy as I've ever been, I'd just received confirmation from Doc. Mathers that my heart wasn't going to keep me alive much longer. He said I should quit drinking, avoid eating anything worthwhile, and install you in a bedroom as far away from me as humanly possible. Of course, I told him to go to hell.

The legal document enclosed is my last will and testament. Get Joe to fly Monroe up from New York, to explain it to you. Basically you get it all, but let the old boy help you. I trust him implicitly; he'll always steer you in the right direction.

Most importantly, if you can bear it, please stay at Harrington Hall. I so want it filled with laughter, noisy children, and all the things I missed. I know there is someone out there for you, and given time, love will find a way back into your life. In fact, cast your mind back to Travers Day. I saw how that young Clemmons looked at you. Marry someone honest and hardworking, Em, someone who adores you like I do and have lots of children.

Oh, I almost forgot, there's some cash. Don't quote me, but I think it's around one hundred and twenty five million dollars, which should keep you occupied for a while.

Have fun, my dearest almost-wife. Now…I don't want any tears. That's an order! Take our horses and the dogs up to Lake Point, and hoist a glass for me because you know in spirit, I'll be there. Go on—go right now. And for the record, though I never got to say this, damn it, I'm doing it now. I love you, dear wife. You were my heart and soul. Eternity is not long enough to thank you for being you, and being there. I love you truly, truly dear, now and forever and a year.

Ever and always, your devoted husband Bill.

P.S. Open the purple box. I'm just sorry I couldn't get you on board sooner.

Fighting back tears, Emily picked up the purple box, and running her fingers over the fine velvet, she flicked up the small gold clasp. Two exquisite platinum and diamond wedding bands nestled inside, and taking the smaller of the two, Emily slipped it on her finger. With Bill's usual attention to detail, it was a perfect fit. She kissed the ring sitting snugly against her trembling finger, and couldn't hold back tears. But twirling the band seemed to have a calming effect, and with Bill's words echoing in her head, Emily composed herself. She rang Brothers to meet her at the front door with a bottle of champagne, and called Max to have her horse saddled, and Bill's Commander on a lead halter.

• • •

When Emily entered what had been Bill's bedroom, it was strange not to have him waiting in his mahogany chair. And the room had a vibe she'd not noticed before. Kicking off her shoes, she opened the closet where their riding gear hung, to find a large sheet of paper hanging from the ceiling. Nervously holding the paper aside, Emily saw none of Bill's clothes. Women's shirts, dresses, skirts, and suits had replaced them. Even in death, he was thinking what she might need, and had taken care of every detail. Fingering the luxurious fabrics of the beautiful clothes the closet now contained, Emily reached for her riding clothes, and on the same hanger as her jodhpurs, discovered the old cashmere waistcoat Bill always wore when he rode. Brushing the familiar fabric against her cheek, she was again aware of his cologne, and realized why he'd left the waistcoat with her things. She pulled on her jodhpurs and boots, topped them with a pale yellow polo sweater, and slipped on Bill's waistcoat. Feeling an indescribable calm, Emily headed downstairs.

Chapter Seventeen

Fall in upstate New York is an explosion of color, as the reds, oranges and yellows of dying foliage compete for glory with the vibrant greens of the steadfast conifers. Emily hurried to the stables knowing September's chill would soon upstage the warmth of the afternoon sun.

Entering the yard, Max was waiting with the horses. Bill's stallion sensed Emily's arrival and pawed the ground impatiently. Then as the dogs entered the yard, bounding up to their equine friends, her young mare began to fidget. Speaking softly to both animals, Max left them standing passively, and tendered his condolences to Emily. Then after giving her a leg-up on her mare and placing Commander's halter in her hand, he watched the trio head to Lake Point.

With the warming rays of the noonday sun overhead, the mare trotted along with the big Lipizzaner by her side. As they crossed the fairway running down to the lake, the presence of several small hazards left for Bill's golfing buddies, reminded Emily of the laughter in his voice when he instructed the groundskeeper to leave each steaming pile where it was. And remembering his silliness, caused an unexpected warmth to flood over her.

Moving on, the mown grass deepened into rough and after a short walk through the woods, Emily pulled to a halt in the glade by the waterfall.

Bright beams of afternoon sun sliced through the woods canopy. And beside the stream babbling over mossy rocks, a clump of pink and white orchids, looking like tiny birds in flight, had forced their way through the rich soil. Emily realized she hadn't noticed flowers before. Now, as she looked around, there were hundreds of the delicate little blooms, reaching toward the fingers of sunlight.

Sliding from the mare, Emily removed the blanket from the back of her saddle and laid it under 'their' tree. Then handing each horse a carrot, she set the rest onto the ground. She smiled as their obscenely loud munching interrupted the glade's quiet, then she opened the more-than-a-little disturbed bottle of champagne. Gasping at the volcanic outpouring of the pale amber liquid, she let a good deal of the Bollinger explosively discharge to the glade floor, and poured a glass from the remains. Then leaning back against the tree where she and Bill had so often made love, she hoisted a glass of champagne to his memory. With the fizzy nectar spattering her nose, Emily drained her glass, and left the bottle in the cool waters of the flowing stream. The glade fairies deserved a drink on Bill too, and kissing her fingertips, she placed them tenderly on the tree, and headed back to Harrington.

Once Emily cleared the woods and crossed the fairway, she could see the front of the house. A car she didn't recognize was parked there.

Chapter Eighteen

When Emily entered the main reception room, two police officers were pacing. It could have been an intimidating scenario, but Brothers had cleverly put them in the room where Emily's position was firmly established by her portrait above the fireplace.

Withdrawing their identity cards, Officers Minnelli, and O'Brian introduced themselves. No sooner had they sat than Brothers appeared with coffee and cookies, and poured everyone a cup.

"So, gentlemen," said Emily, "what can I do for you?"

The officers appeared reticent to say anything with Brothers present, but when he discreetly retired to a position near the door, and it was obvious Emily wasn't going to dismiss him, Minnelli spoke.

"Ms. Wilks, Mr. Brothers here told us of your loss, and you have our condolences. We are sorry to intrude at so sad a time, but we need to ask you some questions about your roommate Judith Cameron."

A flash of The Hermitage crossed Emily's mind. "I'll be happy to help in any way I can."

Minnelli nodded and consulted his notebook. "I'd like to clarify a few details. You and Ms. Cameron work in the cargo warehouse of Transcontinental Airlines, and live at 2D Houston and Vine, Kew Gardens, New York. Is that correct?"

"Not exactly. She works at Transcontinental. I have taken on the responsibility of running this estate. She lives in the Kew apartment alone, and this is my home."

A satisfied twitch crossed Brothers lips.

"So let's get the details straight," said Minnelli. "Up until recently, Ms. Cameron and you worked and lived together."

"Correct, but we were on opposite shifts. We rarely saw each other."

"Did you socialize?"

"I believe I just told you we rarely saw each other."

"So are you saying you know nothing about the theft of twenty-six million dollars in diamonds from the Transcontinental vault?" snapped O'Brian.

"Excuse me, the what?" asked a startled Emily.

"When did you last have any contact with Judith Cameron?" asked Minnelli.

Emily's body language indicated she was rattled.

"Did you hear the question, Ms. Wilks?" pressed O'Brian. "What do you know about the robbery, and where is Judith Cameron?"

Emily was having a hard time focusing on the questions, and formulating an answer. Her mind had frozen on 'the theft of twenty-six million dollars'. When she did speak, it came out as a nervous mumble. "Nothing, I know nothing about a robbery. I haven't seen Jude for days, a week maybe. I don't remember."

Turning as the police often did, to a good cop/bad cop routine, the pair questioned and cajoled Emily for information about Jude's whereabouts and lifestyle. It was several minutes before she stood, and headed for the window. Despite having her back to them, the questions didn't stop, and as her hand nervously twirled her wedding ring, their constant barrage began to intimidate her.

When Brothers discreetly coughed, Emily recognized his support. It shook her into action, and she turned to face the policemen. "Am I to assume, Officer O'Brian, that you suspect I was involved in this robbery?"

O'Brian smiled and said nothing.

"You tell us," said Minnelli with a self-satisfied smirk. "But think about this. Weren't you involved in locating a misplaced diamond shipment belonging to, er, Walvis Bay Holdings, several weeks ago?"

"Yes, but—"

"So it wouldn't be outside the realms of possibility to imagine that that incident was an attempt at robbery, which for whatever reason you and Cameron decided to abort," cut in O'Brian.

"That's absurd," snapped Emily.

"Weren't you and Judith Cameron two of a handful of agents who had security clearance and full access to the Transcontinental vault?" asked Minnelli.

"Yes."

O'Brian cut in again. "So, having that clearance you would both have intimate knowledge that a major shipment was incoming from Walvis Bay Holdings."

"The stolen shipment was from Walvis Bay?" asked Emily.

O'Brian smirked. "Like you didn't know that."

"I most certainly did not know. I have had no contact with anyone from the office since I gave my notice."

Minnelli moved towards her. "And that moves me to the next point."

"Which is?" asked Emily.

"Isn't it unusual for someone without a college education, earning the sort of money you did at Transcontinental, to just up and quit a job for no apparent reason?"

Emily flushed. "I have a reason."

"Twenty-six million reasons?" asked O'Brian.

"Now you're being ridiculous!" Emily countered.

"So why don't you tell us about the other shipment from Walvis Bay Holdings. The one that went missing that no one else at Transcontinental could find."

"It was mislabeled and cataloged incorrectly in the vault. I have a good memory, noticed the numbering sequence was wrong and located it."

"Though we are told several other agents looked, only you could locate it. How convenient."

"What exactly are you implying, Officer O'Brian?"

"What about the helicopter that taxies you about? According to your colleagues you were picked up on a regular basis, and none of them knew where you were going or with whom you were spending time."

Emily smiled thinly. "Just because I don't flaunt my personal life doesn't make me party to a crime. If you had taken a minute to check your facts, you would know I do not own a car, and the helicopter, which is parked out back, belongs to my companion. He was instrumental in me quitting my job."

"And your *companion* would be?" asked O'Brian sarcastically.

"Bill Bailey. Of course, Brothers told you he just died."

Minnelli rubbed his chin. "He just said Mr. Bailey; it could've been anybody."

"Well it wasn't *anybody*. My companion was Bill Bailey."

"The *fifty*-something multi-millionaire?"

"I don't like your tone, Officer Minnelli."

"Just an observation."

"Well you can keep your snide observations to yourself. I have used Bill's helicopter to visit him here for over three years. I would have thought the least you could have done is come here having researched some general information about our friendship. As far as a robbery is concerned, I know absolutely nothing. Judith Cameron and I might have lived in the same apartment, but we had minimal contact with each other. And since my recent trip to Europe, I haven't said two words to her."

"And why would that be, Miss Wilks?" asked O'Brian. "Could something have happened you don't want to tell us about?"

Emily blushed. "I think I have clarified my position on Ms. Cameron."

Minnelli sensed Emily was holding back. "Look Miss, you and Cameron were roommates. You have to know what she did in her spare time, must have overheard a phone call, or taken a cryptic message. Maybe you noted some change in her personality or circumstances that might have prompted her involvement in the theft?"

"Frankly, I neither knew nor cared what she did in her spare—or any other—time. However, I will tell you that since the death of her companion Tina Brazier, she changed considerably, and not for the better. Now is that all, gentlemen? I have things to attend to."

"No, Ms. Wilks, that is not all," said an exasperated O'Brian. "Stop playing with us. We want specific information about Cameron. Where did she gamble? How much did she owe? Who paid the tab? Did she sell drugs?" The edge to his voice was transparently intended to harass Emily. "What was the name of the gentleman you had dinner with in Monaco?"

Emily froze. "That's none of your business."

"Ordinarily, I might agree. But when a cargo handler and the disgruntled son of a diamond merchant get together, and twenty-six million dollars in diamonds goes missing, alarms go off."

"You are so off base I can't even qualify that remark with an—"

O'Brian raised an accusatory eyebrow. "Why did you and Cameron leave a woman to die in Monaco, Miss Wilks?"

The panic on Emily's face was clear. "I have absolutely nothing else to say. I suggest if either of you has any further questions, you direct them to my lawyers. Brothers will give you their card on the way out."

Minnelli looked at O'Brian and nodded. He knew they had pushed as far as they could. "Well, thank you for your time Miss. Wilks. It goes without saying you should not leave the area." He reached into his pocket. "Here's my card, I would appreciate a call if Ms. Cameron contacts you."

Chapter Nineteen

When Emily called Bill's lawyers, she was connected to Harold Monroe, the older of the two partners. Since hearing of Bill's death, he was expecting her call, and while he assumed she wanted to talk about the contents of Bill's will, he was surprised when she asked for advice about the tragic incidents in her past. He listened intently while Emily outlined her suspicions about Jude Cameron's involvement in the events, and admitted her subsequent failure to report those misgivings to the police. Attorney Monroe gave her no immediate opinions, but told her the firm's criminal lawyer Susan Parks would join him when he attended Harrington Hall.

After hanging up, Emily had barely taken a breath when the phone rang. It was Jack.

"What can I say, I am so sorry," he said. "Jaime told me what happened, and I had to call to find out if you're okay."

"I am, thank you. But I'm really busy right now."

"I imagine you must be." Jack's voice quieted. "What did the police have to say to you?"

"How do you know they were here?"

"They told me, and as we speak, they're in Jaime's morning room."

"Why do they want to talk to Jaime?"

"They don't," said Jack. "They came to see me. They think I'm in here calling my father for advice. What gives?"

Emily hesitated. "They knew we met in Monaco."

"They mentioned that. But the police are omnipresent over there, and that murder involving your roommate totally freaked them out."

"I'm not sure Monaco is these particular policemen's primary concern."

"Then what?"

"It seems they think the three of us are in cahoots to steal your father's diamond shipment."

"Judith Cameron stole our shipment?"

"That's what they tell me."

"And you and I are working with her?" asked Jack. "That's ridiculous."

"I said as much. But putting certain things together, anyone hearing their side of the story could easily think it's true."

"So do they know where she is?"

"No," said Emily. "But they think I do."

"You told me you've had nothing to do with her since Monaco."

"I haven't, nor do I care where she is."

"Emily, think. You lived with her." Concern gave an edge to Jacks' voice. "She can clear your name—damn it, our names; you must have some idea where she went."

"Not you, too. Look, Jack, you might be concerned about my welfare, but I'm fine. And right now all I want to do is carry out Bill's last wishes with some dignity before a media circus descends on Harrington Hall."

"Yes, Em, I'm sorry."

"Don't call me that."

"You mean Em?"

"Yes."

"Why?"

"That's what Bill called me."

"Damn, could I be any more insensitive? Emily, I'm worried about you. I need to see you."

"That is simply not possible, Jack. Best you go back to South Africa and forget me."

"Just like that. Now who's being insensitive?"

"It's all I can muster right now."

"Well, I'm not going down quietly," said Jack. "After our last conversation at Saratoga, I called my father and we spoke to his lawyers."

"I have lawyers. I don't need your help." Emily's voice hardened. "And I certainly don't need to be beholden to your father."

"He can have the Monaco police confirm where we were while all the mayhem was going on."

"It's just one overly protective father's word."

"Not exactly."

"What do you mean?" asked Emily.

"The cameras, on every street corner. We're on film somewhere."

"So? We don't know when the murder happened. And when you say you want to help someone suspected of being involved in murder and stealing his diamonds, he'll tell you to walk away."

"You don't know that," said Jack adamantly.

"Sticking up for me will simply confirm his feelings that you're irresponsible."

"Three years ago; but not now. Apparently, he'd been waiting years for me to get a spine and prove I can do something other than be a tour guide for his guests. Me following you to America; tying up with Jaime and getting a job in the city, all convinced him I'm on the right track to make something of myself. And at least he won't be able to call you a gold digger. Jaime tells me Bill left you a great deal of money."

"It's meaningless without him. So how's your job going?"

"I've been offered V.P. International Acquisitions."

"Good, I'm glad for you," said Emily. "Now you can start a new life, settle down, and do all those things you talked about."

"Will you be there?"

"Me—why?"

"Emily, don't be stupid. You know how I feel about you."

"My closest friend just died, I haven't said my goodbyes yet and you want to talk about an 'us' that doesn't exist?"

"I know my timing stinks, but you're wrong. You know what *exists* between us and I'm not giving up on you."

"I can see there is nothing I can say to persuade you otherwise, so go ahead, look into the dumb things I've done, and then tell me you want to be with me. In the meantime, I'm too upset for this nonsense. I'm hanging up now, but remember one thing—dont underestimate those policemen. This is not South Africa and your father's influence does not stretch this far."

"I need to see you, Emily."

"Sorry, Jack, that's just not appropriate."

"I'm through with that."

"Through with what?" asked Emily.

"Always doing what is appropriate."

For the second time in a week, Emily hung up the phone and sobbed.

Chapter Twenty

It was close to three o'clock when Emily came downstairs, and as she entered the garden room, friends were already sipping champagne, and munching on a buffet. It was no surprise to her that Bill had pre-arranged his wake. As she circulated the room, it comforted her that the friends knew about the velvet box, and were delighted she was honoring Bill's unfulfilled dream, by wearing the wedding band he had left for her. And no one was surprised he left his fortune to her.

• • •

When the gathering broke up at six, Emily was alone with the distant ticking and mournful chimes of a grandfather clock. Solitary and pensive, she could feel an empty silence descend upon the house. And as she walked around the room, picking up a glass here and a dish there, she agonized about what was expected of her.

Thanks to Bill, she would never want for anything again, but unless she could put the demons of her past to rest, the thing she wanted most was inappropriate to have. Pinching herself sharply for bemoaning her lot, Emily knew her selfish issues were unimportant in the bigger scheme of things. Bill had entrusted her with his empire, and no matter how hard she had to work, she would do whatever was necessary to keep it alive.

• • •

By mid-evening, Emily was in the study, sunk deep in Bill's chair, wading through papers. The list of companies she now owned spanned the globe, and as she scanned the pages of seemingly endless weekly reports, Emily got a small taste of how Bill occupied his time. When Brothers disturbed her, it was to show in her new lawyer, Susan Parks.

"Ms. Wilks," said the young lawyer, proffering her hand. "It's so nice to finally meet you. Mr. Bailey spoke often of you."

"Really; please call me Emily and you are Susan?"

"I am," Susan said. "Now, I know from the conversation you had with Mr. Monroe, you have some pressing personal concerns to talk about."

"Will you be handling the business side of things?"

"No, my area of expertise is criminal law."

"Is that what I am, a criminal?"

"I don't know yet. Often seemingly serious indiscretions in the past aren't nearly as bad when you talk them through. So, let's hear what you've got."

Emily smiled. "I'm so relieved I can finally tell someone else about everything stupid I've done. Bill knew most of it and if he were here, he would talk to the authorities and clarify everything. With him gone, I'm not even sure where to start."

"I find the beginning is good."

"Of course," said Emily. "Sorry, I'm a little nervous. Apart from Bill there is one other person I've talked to. But the more I think about him, the more vulnerable I feel."

"Who is that, and why would you feel vulnerable?"

Emily's eyes scanned the floor. "It's a friend I made in Monaco… er…Jack Clemmons."

"Is he a boyfriend-type of a friend, or a 'see you when I see you' friend?" Susan knew she'd hit a nerve when Emily blushed. "Don't answer if you're uncomfortable. We can talk about him later. Do you mind if I take notes?"

"No, that's fine."

As Susan typed steadily into her laptop, Emily outlined her financial and emotional difficulties after the deaths of her parents and grandmother. She also relayed that it was Jude Cameron and Tina Brazier who'd informally adopted her, sharing their home and resources, until she joined Transcontinental Airlines cargo department.

"In the beginning, Jude and Tina were wonderful parents," said Emily. "We had airline passes so we traveled abroad together. They introduced me to new experiences, and told me things about love and life that my real parents probably never would. And above all, they encouraged me to be open to people's differences."

"Differences?" asked Susan.

"Didn't I say they were gay? Does that matter?"

"I don't know, but treat me like your priest. Even though what you say might seem unimportant, try and include everything. In my experience, it's often the insignificant details that mount up, and sort out the problem."

"Okay, so the most important lesson to be learned living with Jude and Tina was tolerance."

Susan raised an eyebrow. "Oh?"

"They drank, gambled, and used drugs, and as I had a small trust fund for my education, they asked if they could borrow a few dollars here and there to pay debts."

"You mean they stole it."

"No. They asked for my help, and I gave it."

"Did you get to use any of the money for your education?"

"Not really," said Emily.

"Did they pay the money back?"

"Not exactly."

"So they stole it."

"Absolutely not. They were raising me. It was the least I could do. Besides, they took me places. I went on a lot of trips until I became involved in a couple of awkward situations."

Susan stopped typing. "What do you mean, 'awkward situations'?"

"One incident occurred when Jude and I were driving out to Bear Mountain. She said she knew a fun campsite to spend the night. It was a mess, full of broken-down trailers, Winnebagos, and VW vans, and I wanted to head home. But it suited her because it had a makeshift pot shop and booze house. We tied up with a bunch of hikers looking for a party, and when I wanted out, Jude started whining about me being an uptight, ungrateful brat. So I joined in the drinking."

"Were you and the hikers underage?"

Emily nodded.

"That's no big whoop, Emily. Not that I condone youngsters boozing it up, but it's really no big deal."

"That's not the point of the story."

"Sorry, go on."

"After three glasses of wine," continued Emily, "I'd had my fill. But the others wanted to finish off the booze and add marijuana to the mix. I draw the line at drugs, left them, and headed off to a local motel. Next thing I know, the desk clerk is waking me saying Jude is collapsed in a bleeding heap on the reception floor."

"How did she know where you were?"

"There's nothing else around. You just walk down the road from the campsite and there's the motel. She knew I was headed there."

"Did you call an ambulance?"

"No she wouldn't have it. The desk clerk helped me get her in bed to sleep it off. In the morning, she woke up looking like death warmed over and we went home."

Susan shrugged. "I don't see anything untoward so far."

Emily took a deep breath. "When we got to the apartment, I left Jude and went out to get peroxide and bandages. I also picked up the evening edition of the newspaper. The front page was full of an accident on Bear Mountain. Four people were killed right where we were. It said the police suspected the younger pair had crossed the centerline and hit another oncoming car head-on, and that alcohol and drugs had contributed to the crash. Also evidence at the scene indicated another person had been ejected from the youngster's truck bed, but no body was found."

"And why should that bother you so much?"

"Because the kids pictured in the newspaper were the kids Jude had been drinking and smoking weed with. And she came to the motel looking like she'd been run over by a tank."

"That doesn't mean she was with them."

"But I asked her—she was."

"Oh."

"Yes, oh," said Emily. "I wanted to call the cops, but Jude got all threatening. She was talking about underage drinking and me being an accessory after the fact. How much I owed her for taking me in off the street, and what would happen if she went to jail. I was a kid, I froze."

"And where was Jude's companion, Tina, during all this."

"Buying drugs with my rent check."

"Oh, this just gets better and better."

"I told you. But she didn't get home with the drugs. She was struck by a hit-and-run driver crossing Westlake. And I knew who did it."

"So you told the cops."

"I couldn't. A guy named Alberto came to the apartment, muscled money out of Jude, and told us Tina got what she deserved for trying to cheat him. And if we said anything to anybody, we'd be dead right alongside her."

Susan stopped typing. "Well, Emily, I have to tell you, this is not looking good. If what you're saying checks out—and I have no doubt it will—we have some major obstruction of justice issues. You need some serious alibis here. Bill's not here to help but Jude Cameron should be able to clear up certain things. Is she still living at the apartment in Kew?"

"They didn't tell you?"

"They?"

"The police. They were here earlier and suspect Jude has absconded with twenty-six million dollars in diamonds from the Transcontinental warehouse. And they think I'm in on the robbery with her."

"Why would they think that?"

"Because I haven't yet told you about what she did in Monaco or my friend Jack Clemmons."

"The guy you mentioned earlier?"

Emily nodded. "In the cop's words, he's not only my friend, but the disgruntled son of the owner of the diamonds."

"Holy crap!"

Chapter Twenty-One

Jack would have preferred not to return to southwest Africa. However, dealing with his father's lawyers by phone, e-mail, and Skype was driving him to distraction. Apart from poor reception, the time difference and delays in getting answers to his questions, it seemed every time he felt an avenue of clarification presented itself, another fork in the road appeared. So after three weeks of uncovering more questions than answers, he attended the Windhoek offices of de Jong, Olembe and Obote, his father's lawyers.

"Well, hello young Clemmons," said de Jong, extending a hand. "We finally received word from the American authorities regarding the films from Monaco's police department."

"And?"

"Your father has presented the evidence and spoken to the authorities about you and Ms. Wilks being involved in the Dutch woman's murder. The point is now moot. Further, his testimony vis-a-vis your role in Walvis Bay Holdings, your whereabouts prior to the theft from Transcontinental, and the details of your personal inheritance, have allayed any suspicion they might have about your involvement in the robbery."

"Emily too?"

"Not so much. According to the Americans; she was in the right location immediately prior to the robbery, knew the alleged players well, and had sufficient motive to assist in the theft. Clearly, it's going to take a lot more work to clear her."

"That's what you're being paid to do."

"Quite, but draw in those horns and take a look at this." De Jong pushed a file across to Jack. "The Americans were very forthcoming sharing their information with us. And having studied this, I am of the opinion that Ms. Wilks's involvement in the robbery is a stretch. But there is no doubt she is somewhat a victim of circumstance. To proceed any further in helping her, those circumstances must be clarified."

"That's about as convoluted as any lawyer can make it. She was with me or her friend Bill, before, during and after the robbery. Talk to Bailey's staff; compare timelines on the Monaco films. Look at the Transcontinental warehouse surveillance footage."

The lawyer smiled benevolently. "We haven't been sitting on our hands these past weeks, young Clemmons. But this is Africa, and the power to progress is in American hands. We can only come at this dilemma from the point of view of the diamond theft. If we'd have pushed too hard regarding Ms. Wilks personally, they'd have shut us out."

"Yes, I understand. I'm sorry. Time seems to be getting away from us and I just feel we're going nowhere."

"Nowhere is pretty harsh, even for a young man with your passion. So, here we are so far. It's clear Ms. Wilks was with you during the incident in Monaco. She is cleared. In regards to Bill Bailey's staff? We are not permitted to approach them without cause. Within the realms of the robbery from JFK, I cannot find one. And there is a problem with surveillance film at Transcontinental. Even the Americans have no evidence of what was happening there."

"You mean the surveillance system was malfunctioning, or they don't have a system?"

"Apparently they don't have a system."

"God almighty," said Jack. "Millions of dollars of merchandise coming and going, and there are no cameras. What was the management thinking?"

"Seems they weren't."

Jack ran a hand through his hair. "But the mere fact that Emily was telling the truth about Monaco—surely that means something."

"Your heart might say so, but the evidence isn't as clear cut. There are anomalies about the roommate situation that the Americans are still looking into."

"Such as?"

"Who knew what, when?"

Jack began to pace. "Now you're just being obtuse. I told you, Emily had come to hate Jude Cameron. The woman started off as a supportive surrogate parent and ended up a money-grubbing monster with a gambling habit."

"Of that we are sure. And according to the records, Ms. Wilks paid Cameron's debts several times."

"I know that. But given the circumstances, surrogate parent and all, wouldn't any daughter help if she could?"

"It's called enabling."

Jack couldn't hide his frustration. "Well, thank you for making Emily sound like a total accomplice."

"These are the facts."

"Well I'm ignoring you on *the facts*. Move to the present. If Cameron took our diamonds, how did she get away from JFK?"

"The authorities suspect she worked with a cargo pilot called T.W. Ford at the behest of a group of individuals that even we are not prepared to tackle."

"You mean—like the mafia?"

The lawyer smiled. "Let's just say the Americans are laying the actual robbery squarely on the shoulders of Cameron and the cargo pilot Ford. However, though Miss Wilks is not concretely allied to the theft, they are still wrestling with her admission that she knew, but said nothing, about Cameron's nefarious dealings."

"You had carte blanche to look into all that," snapped Jack. "I gave you an outline of Emily's past, even told you when I spoke to her at Saratoga. She had suspicions that Cameron was stealing. Suspicions, that's all. She couldn't prove anything."

"We followed up, as did the Americans. Sadly, in Ms. Wilks' line of work, bonded agent and all, it is mandatory that even a suspicion be brought to a superior's attention. It was not."

"So what do we do now?" asked a disgruntled Jack.

"Nothing. We have gone about as far as we can go. According to our sources, at the very minimum, she will be charged with five counts of obstruction of justice."

"Five? Where did five come from? She mentioned Jude Cameron and three shipments to me."

"There are other incidents."

Jack dropped heavily into a chair. "Will she go jail?"

"It seems likely."

"Then get her off."

Lawyer de Jong quietly closed the file. "We are in no position to do that."

"Why? You kept me from jail, and my charges were way more serious."

"You were here in South Africa. We have different rules, different influences at work. She will have to serve her time unless she is freed on appeal."

"Then I have to go back right away, and find a way to help her with that."

De Jong took off his glasses. "Is that something you father will approve of?"

"I don't give a damn what he approves of, I'm going back to America. With or without his permission, I have to do what's right."

"Then you should probably have this." De Jong pushed a portfolio across the desk alongside Emily's file. "It's the inheritance from your mother."

"I thought my father retained control of that until I'm thirty."

"Apparently he petitioned a judge to release it now. According to the application, you have become qualified to handle it."

Jack opened the file. "Jesus, fifty million dollars. I thought it was a small inheritance?"

"To your father, it is. Now, young man, that other file contains copies of all the information we amassed, as well as your ticket back to New York."

Jack flipped open the file. "My father had you do this, too?"

De Jong smiled. "Study that information, because if you're determined to help minimize Ms. Wilk's sentence, you should know what you're getting yourself into."

"She told me everything I need to know."

"Maybe, but take the file and a piece of advice from an old man. Don't cut your father out of your life. Read and learn something from Ms. Wilks's actions."

"And what might that be?"

"Some people aren't cut out to be parents; that doesn't make them any less family. Do the best you can with whomever you're given."

Chapter Twenty-Two

As she continued to talk to her attorney, Emily's emotions were laid bare. Her gut always told her the events of her past might one day haunt her, but she had no idea her acts of omission could so drastically conspire to shape her future.

"So, Emily," said Susan. "It's clear Jude Cameron was into some pretty dodgy things. Why didn't you say something to the authorities about your suspicions?"

"Because they were just that, I had no proof. Besides, she was the closest thing I had to family. You don't welch on the person who raised you. And even if I wanted to distance myself, I still had to live with her at Kew. I couldn't afford an apartment of my own."

"But you knew Bill by this time."

"Thank God. He was my savior."

"He'd have given you money for an apartment."

"I know," said Emily. "He offered, a jillion times. But that's just not me. I work out my own problems, and I didn't want anybody saying I was only with him for his money. On reflection, I wished I'd have taken his offer. And you know what's really ironic. The guys in the lunchroom were always talking about the lousy security at Transcon'. How with an airplane ready, all you needed to do was jog onto the tarmac, and you could be away with a million bucks in gems before anyone realized you were gone. Who knew she'd actually do it?"

"You're sure she did it, then?"

Emily nodded. "She told me as much on the way back from Monaco. Sober, she was guarded about everything. After several glasses of wine—*in vino veritas*—the floodgates opened. Naturally, I thought she was doing her usual drunken bragging. Who knew for once she was telling the truth."

"Did she indicate anyone else at the warehouse might be involved?"

"No. Besides, from what the cops said, everybody else is still there—except me. I can see how they might think I was involved, and in some way I suppose I am."

"Now that's a damning statement. Care to explain it?"

"I'm an intelligent person so I have no excuse. In my usual fashion, I simply chose to ignore the signs."

"Signs?" asked Susan.

"Before she actually told me what she was going to do, there were hang-ups and dead air when I answered the phone. She would be huddled in a corner of the warehouse with guys who looked like gangsters. There'd be screaming matches because I wouldn't change a shift with her."

"Did anything specific happen before the diamonds to let you categorically know she was stealing?"

"Stuff started to disappear from the warehouse."

"Did you actually see her take anything?"

"No, she was far too clever. And, anyway, I really didn't want it to be true. You have to understand; when I was younger, she was like my parent. She and Tina saved me from being a ward of the state. From being assigned to foster care or an orphanage. Hadn't she earned a measure of loyalty for taking me in after my real family died? Didn't I owe her the benefit of doubt? "

Susan smiled thinly. "My heart says you did what most family would do. But I'm not sure a court of law will be entirely on the same page. Now let's get closer to today. Tell me about the incident in Monaco."

There was a knock, and the study door opened. "Beg pardon, miss," said Brothers. "It's ten P.M.; would you like anything before I retire?"

Emily looked at Susan. "White wine good for you? I'll need something to get me through Monaco."

"Whatever keeps the wheels rolling."

"Thank you, Brothers, chardonnay would be nice and something to nibble on, if Mrs. Hudson has anything made."

"She does, miss. And pardon me for saying, but she's worried about you, and wanted me to say, 'don't you be up all night chatting'."

Emily smiled at Brothers' impression of Mrs. Hudson.

Brothers quickly returned with the wine, and a platter of Emily's favorite canapés. And after pouring them each a glass of chilled chardonnay, he discreetly retired.

"The staff thinks a lot of you," said Susan.

Emily took a sip of the wine. "Which will make it all the more difficult when they find out I'm a complete failure as a human being."

"That's a bit harsh. How about we take one step at a time. Now, Monaco, from the beginning."

"I was attending an airline awards dinner, and when Jude found out it was in Monaco, she begged to bum a share of my room for a couple of days. I said okay, because I was trying to get along, and I knew she was only there to go to the casino. She was going to use her latest 'system'. As you can imagine, she gambled, and lost, a lot. I even bailed her out a few times. Anyway, she turned up from Geneva with over $25,000 in Swiss francs, which she said she won at their tables."

As the golden liquid relaxed her, Emily relayed the details of Jude's arrival in Monaco, and how she lost all her money, which gave way to a violent outburst and her intimidating behavior at The Hermitage's reception. Then on the flight home, when Emily finally got Jude to explain their abrupt departure, she was horrified to learn Jude was running from Monaco after attacking a young woman.

"But you did nothing about it when you got back to the states?" asked Susan.

"Nothing. I wrote it off as more of Jude's crap and moved on."

"You really didn't know the true consequence of that argument until Jack Clemmons told you?"

"I did not."

"But after you knew Jude had committed a murder, you still said nothing to the police?"

Emily looked down. "I'm not proud of that."

"So tell me about Jack Clemmons."

Emily topped off their glasses. "Bill was incredible to me, Susan. He would have given me the world. However, over the past few months, we've had a difficult time. You probably know Bill was twenty-six years older than me, and although he was really fit, the differences in our age had really started to show. I wanted to go out and do things, be spontaneous, and totally outrageous, which I couldn't be in Bill's circle. He was content to trade dinners at home with his friends."

"So when he continued to ask you to marry him, you were torn?"

"I was. Plus, I knew he couldn't have children, and he didn't want to adopt. It didn't bother me at first because, he is—*was*—so special. Then as thirty quickly approached, I'm embarrassed to admit, I didn't want to spend the rest of my life with just him. Both Bill and I came from small families. And though he had an older brother, I had no siblings. Neither did I really know the family I had. Those still alive after my immediate family died were in Ireland. It sounds selfish, but I wanted a houseful of kids. I had to grow up so fast I barely remember what being a kid was like. I wanted to be part of a proper family. I wanted births and christenings, weddings and family cookouts on the Fourth of July. I wanted to be part of something bigger than just Bill and me. God, I sound so selfish; why would he even put up with me?"

Susan smiled. "Because, despite his limitations, you made him feel needed, and loved. There's also no doubt in my mind that mutual devotion was there, because despite being torn, you stood by him until the end. So, where does Clemmons come in?"

"Actually through work; I found his father's diamond shipment, which was ostensibly lost."

"*Ostensibly* lost?"

"Nobody could find it, and we were about to register an insurance claim. Then Jack called me."

"Did you know him before?"

"No. I'd helped track down something for one his business colleagues and he was given my name. Anyway, I looked into Jack's shipment and found it had been misplaced, wrongly documented, call it what you will. And in the course of our conversation I said something like, his timing was perfect, because I was about to leave for an airline awards dinner in Monaco. He said he was in the Mediterranean and if he happened to be there too, could he buy me a thank-you dinner."

"So, you made a date."

"No, I would never go behind Bill's back," said Emily. "It was one of those things you say to a customer. He or she says, 'thank you so much, I owe you dinner,' and you say okay. It's happened a thousand times. I've never actually followed through."

"But you did with Jack."

"I told you. Bill and I were having some issues. Well no, that's not strictly true, *I* was having some issues. But our meeting was innocent. I was staying at The Hermitage, where Jack sometimes stays and we got chatting. Nothing untoward happened during or after dinner, except we got on like a house on fire. We were so on the same wavelength, I felt I'd known him all my life, and he thought the same about me. We laughed about our travel misadventures, and talked about politics and religion. I ask you, politics and religion. Does that sound like a date?"

"No. But you clearly made an impression."

"And he did on me," said Emily. "He's a very nice guy. But not enough to do anything that would hurt Bill. Anyway, by the time I got back to the States, Jude's antics had made up my mind. I didn't want any more to do with her. Also, I finally realized I had no right to keep a wonderful man like Bill hanging on any longer. So, I decided to simply leave the apartment and move in with him."

"But you met Jack Clemmons again here."

"By accident; Bill and I ran into him at the Saratoga races. At first, I couldn't understand why he was in America. Then he said he wanted to make sure I was all right."

"All right?" asked Susan.

"The people at The Hermitage told him I'd been beaten up and he was worried about me. That's when he told me Jude not only attacked that young woman, but left her to die. I lost it. I had to lie to Bill and told him an acquaintance Jack and I knew had died. And while Jack didn't say anything out of place, I now know Bill saw something more than the death of an acquaintance between us." Emily handed Susan Bill's letter. "Here, look at this."

The attorney's eyes misted as she read, and the look she gave Emily ate into her soul. "This is a beautiful affirmation of how he felt about you."

"I really loved him, Susan, and somehow knew we would have a short time together. I tried to make that time the most fun I could. Why didn't he just tell me how sick he was?"

"Because he loved you and didn't want to burden you."

"Now he's gone, and left me everything. I'm not his wife; I don't deserve a penny of it."

"That's nonsense and you know it," said Susan. "Listen to me. It's quite clear that he looked upon you as Mrs. Bailey. You weren't able to legally accomplish that, but we both know it would have happened. Anyone who reads this letter will know Bill knew that, too, and no amount of doubt or regret is going to change that. But I'm not here to ponder what might have been. As Bill would want, I'm here to get you out of a jam." Susan put the letter in the copy machine. "For now, I'll take a copy of the letter. However, I do remember it says you are not to cry. So, dry up those tears. You know Bill Bailey always got what he wanted."

Emily blotted her eyes. "Thank you for listening, Susan. I feel so much better."

"Good. And hopefully you realize had you not felt such an obligation to Jude Cameron, much of what transpired wouldn't have happened."

Emily nodded. "So how much trouble am I in?"

"I'm not going to lie. There will probably be some jail time."

"Will anyone else understand that, dysfunctional or not, I was trying to preserve the only family I had?"

"My job is to relay that to the court."

"Okay, you're in control," said Emily. "But I want no excuses made. I will take whatever punishment is just."

"Let's not get ahead of ourselves." Susan connected to the study printer and handed Emily a pile of notes. "Read through these statements for accuracy, and add the names of any people at the airport, who might corroborate your suspicions. Also, list exactly what questions and answers were exchanged with the police officers before I got here."

Emily fanned the pile of notes. "God, what a mess. Will I ever get my life on some sort of normal course?"

"I think so. Look, here's one thing right now that you don't have worry about."

"What's that?"

"Notes on Jude Cameron's accident at Bear Mountain."

"Bear Mountain, when did you get those?"

"Just. I had one of the interns pull Bill's personal file at the office."

"At this time of night?"

"They want to be lawyers," said Susan grinning. "They have to do time, too."

"So what does it say?"

"Seems this goes back to when Bill met you in Fiji. He had to be sure you weren't a gold digger. Then when he found out you lived with Judith Cameron, that you weren't gay. Also, he wanted to find out a little about your past. It's routine for a man in his position to do that, so don't be angry with him."

Emily smiled. "I'm not. It's exactly what I would expect of him. His attention to detail was one of the things I most loved about him."

"So according to this," continued Susan, "he had a private investigator befriend Jude. One night, in the bravado of booze and reefers—"

"Well, she's consistent if nothing else," interrupted Emily.

Susan smiled. "She confessed to leaving the accident scene at Bear Mountain. She also stated that you were asleep at the motel when the accident happened, and it wasn't until a picture of the dead teens appeared in the local paper that you confronted her. She then bragged to the P.I. that you believed the, and I quote here, 'load of horseshit' story she recounted, and no more was said. I have a sworn statement exonerating you, and although you might have approached the police with your suspicions, you were giving Jude the benefit of doubt."

"Bill knew about the whole thing and said nothing to me."

"He clearly felt something for you from the beginning, and wanted to protect you."

"So, I can't be charged over that?"

"According to the file, Bill made a very generous anonymous donation to the victims' families, and with them not driving the investigation for closure, the case seems to have faded away. However, while the compensation may have helped ease Bill's conscience, legally, the case is still open. With him gone, justifying both of you remaining silent is complicated. You're going to have to trust me to sort that out."

"So what happens to Jude?"

"Do you care?" Susan closed the copier lid and hit print.

"At this point, not especially."

"Then let the chips fall where they may."

"It's a pity Bill didn't have someone checking on me in Monaco. I'd have evidence of the time I spent with Jack Clemmons and Jude's vicious behavior towards me. That would back up what I said about her violence and my decision to finally distance myself from her."

"What about Jack Clemmons; let's get him on board."

"I don't know. He called me after the police were here, and wanted to see me. I pretty much told him I didn't want him involved and I could handle things alone. Besides, once his father finds out about my past, I have the distinct feeling Jack Clemmons will be dispatched somewhere far, far, away."

"His father? I know it was his company that lost their diamonds, but how could he influence his grown son against you?"

"Jack got into some trouble in South Africa and his father has run his life since. And from what Jack told me about the senior Clemmons, my actions will pretty much confirm any negative opinions he has about me."

Susan drained her glass. "Well I'm still keeping him on the back burner. For now, I'll have enough work to do. I already know that, as you are airport bonded and security cleared, even without actual proof of wrongdoing, you should have spoken up about your concerns. Alienating a person you looked upon as a parent is a flimsy justification for silence. As for Monaco, you believed what Jude Cameron wanted you to believe. It wasn't until Jack Clemmons re-acquainted himself that you discovered the truth. At that point, you definitely should have gone to the police and told them what you suspected, especially as Jude Cameron's previous activity on Bear Mountain, cast a major shadow over her credibility. Nevertheless, in your defense, I'm going to argue that familial guilt, and Bill dying, overshadowed your thinking. It's weak, but it's the best I have. There are many gaps to fill in, and I'll do everything I can to minimize your punishment."

Emily looked worried. "So how long will I get?"

"I'm not sure, it depends on how good a case I make. In any instance, you'll probably be detained in a minimum security detention center."

"Then will it be over?" asked Emily. "Will I be free?"

"That's up to you. The sentence is a small thing compared to your conscience. To move on with your life, you have to come to terms with the fact that your past, good or bad, has made you the person you are. Whatever you think, you're not a bad person; you just need to be more careful who you trust."

"Thank you, Susan, I don't know what I would've done without you." Emily looked at her watch. "Good grief, its midnight. Let's get to bed. I don't want to wear you out on your first day."

Susan smiled. "Don't worry about me; I'm used to long hours. With the loss of Bill and all, you're the one who needs sleep. Tomorrow, your plate will be full with accountants, so I'm returning to New York. I want a little talk with Officers Minnelli and O'Brian and despite your misgivings I'm going to make my best effort to connect with Jack Clemmons."

Chapter Twenty-Three

During his life, Bill was a spiritual man, but had little time for organized religion. It was fitting therefore, that after a simple cremation, dozens of friends and employees should assemble at the estate for a celebration of life and new beginnings. With the long shadows of October creeping across the links and the forest's leaves lying in crisp golden carpets in the distance, Joe lifted off the helipad. With Emily holding the small copper urn next to her heart, Joe circled the estate with Bill, one last time.

Max had released the horses into the south meadow, and as the helicopter made a low pass over the herd, all save one, scattered to the winds. Bill's big Lipizzaner alone seemed to sense the occasion, and galloped with head and tail at full stretch, beneath the aircraft. He did not break stride until he approached the lake at the far side. There, he dug in his hooves, and skidded to a halt, inches from the water's edge. Then snorting in triumph, the horse regained his footing, and reared up as if to touch the machine overhead.

Had she been in a movie, Emily couldn't have imagined anything so poignant, as the huge white stallion pawing at the air.

The helicopter's rotors kicked up dancing ripples atop the water. And, as Joe tickled the controls to maintain an almost motionless attitude, he nodded at Emily.

Emily kissed the vessel, strangely warm, as if Bill were there, and smiled. She knew her body had generated the heat, but the thought was fitting. She always felt so warm, so safe and so loved with Bill close. Removing the lid, she tilted the urn downward and watched as her almost husband flew with the wind to settle on his beloved estate. And as the last of his ashes swirled beneath the helicopter's downdraft, Emily placed a single red rose into the vessel. The urn was cold now, devoid of his ashes and his essence, and her tears welled. She said a last goodbye and dropped the container into the depths of the rippling lake.

The copper urn shone bright against the water, spiraled twice and sank into the undulating blackness.

...

It was late when the last of their friends departed. And as Emily dragged herself upstairs, kicked her shoes off, and padded into Bill's bedroom, she had the distinct feeling someone had been in there. Looking at the mahogany chair, where she had so often given Bill his favorite lap dance, the seat now held a large black box. It was heavy, tied with gold ribbon, and gave off the expensive fragrance of Chanel.

She smiled, wondering what else Bill had put Brothers up to, and opening the box, she separated the embossed tissue paper to uncover a sable coat. Her trembling hands could barely hold the enclosed card.

> *"Dearest Love, I promise this is the last thing I asked Brothers to spring on you, but I needed to be sure you wouldn't freeze to death in the October mists, while I'm living it up in the warmth of…well…you know where!"*

Emily smiled at Bill's irreverent reference, and picking up the weighty extravagance, she brushed her cheek with the luxurious fullness of the knuckle-deep pelts. As always, Bill's taste was exquisite, and slipping on the coat, his sentiments and its sensuous silkiness enfolded her like warm chocolate.

Chapter Twenty-Four

Jack very badly wanted to attend Bill's funeral. Wanted to hold Emily, and let her know she had his support. Wanted to assure her that whatever difficulty she was in, he'd make it right. But it wasn't time for him to do that. He'd spent sleepless nights thinking about her, and knew one thing for sure. If ever they could be a couple, she must feel free to love him back. It would be difficult, but the only way he could win over Emily was by proving she had nothing to do with the robbery at Transcontinental. He had to find out where Jude Cameron and T.W. Ford went, and get his father's diamonds back.

He picked up the phone and called his father.

"Hi son," said Peter Clemmons sleepily. "It's the middle of the night, where are you?"

"I knew you'd still be up working, I'm in Portland."

"Australia, Jamaica, England, New Zealand, or USA?"

Jack laughed. "USA."

"Indiana, Maine or Oregon?"

"Dad, enough; how do you do that?"

"It's a gift. So need I ask why you're in Portland, Maine?"

"You know what I'm up to most any time," said Jack. "Why should now be any different?"

"Touché—so how can I help?"

"First, thank you for releasing the money."

"It was always yours," said Peter. "But your mother was such a campaigner I just wanted to make sure it was put to good use. By proving you're responsible enough to have a cause, you earned it."

"By 'cause', you mean helping Emily."

"Yes, son. She wouldn't have been my first choice, but—"

Jack's voice hardened. "I didn't call to get your approval. I'm a big boy now so let me handle my life."

"Okay, I get it. What do you need?"

"I want to tap that prodigious memory of yours. When I was working Walvis acquisitions, did I recall a team of investigators here in Maine that you used for a client background check?"

"Yes, Libby and Watterson on Congress Street. They were incredibly thorough, a top notch team."

"Damn, that's right. I couldn't remember their names."

"Quit blowing smoke," said Peter. "Your memory is almost as good as mine. Plus, you could've looked up 'investigators' in the phone book."

"You know, someday I'm going to be one step ahead of you."

Peter Clemmons laughed. "And that's the day I hang up my dancing shoes. I'm assuming you need the team to look into something to help your friend Emily?"

"I want her to be more than a friend, Dad; I'd like to spend the rest of my life with her."

"And does she feel the same way?"

"Not exactly."

"That's going to make getting together complicated."

"I realize that," said Jack.

"You know the insurance company is already working on the whys and wherefores of the Transcontinental case."

"I know, but they're treading water. They're convinced the pilot flew out to sea, and then doubled back to the mainland. It doesn't resonate with me."

"Why not?"

"It's not what I'd do," said Jack.

"And precisely how much thought have you given to a life of crime?"

"What?" said a startled Jack. "I haven't given any thoug—you can't possibly think I'd—"

Peter chuckled. "Jack, stop. Can't a dad tease his son now and again?"

"Sorry. I'm not used to you being—"

"I know. Hopefully, we can change that. I understand how anxious you must be, but insurance investigation does take time."

"I can't bear the thought of Emily rotting in prison because they're moving at a snail's pace. I need to do something now, point somebody in a direction."

"So what progress have you made so far?" asked Peter.

"Obviously you know I was in Windhoek with de Jong. And I've been going over the files he gave me. It seems the pilot suspected of helping Emily's roommate operates from a little airstrip in Sanford, here in Maine. The file made a passing reference to his friendship with a waitress and a group of pilots at the airport café. I figure they might be more forthcoming with answers if the questions were put by a couple of local investigators."

"That's sound reasoning, which is why Walvis always uses locals. I'll make a phone call and authorize anything you want. But why are you there?"

"I want to go along with them," answered Jack. "I have a hunch where the pilot may have headed, and my head is full of questions somebody else wouldn't come up with."

"And where is this hunch coming from?"

"From the notes and what I'd do…don't say anything, Dad. This Ford character's airplane was rigged with additional tanks, which could carry him way further than required for his normal route. The notes also mentioned his dream to run an island hopping charter. But most important, while Ford appears to have the drive and ambition to make his dream a reality, he was held in check by obligation and necessity."

"I can see how that would resonate with you," said Peter.

"I simply feel that once he was committed and headed out to sea, he just kept going. From where he went off radar, straight across as the crow flies is Bermuda. I figure I'd start asking questions there."

"The 'islands' generally means the Bahamas, son."

"I know. But he couldn't make it there. De Jong said the cops and the TSB suspect a major criminal organization planned the robbery; Ford was just pulling flight pay. So, he's not going to do anything suicidal like trying to get to the islands. I think Bermuda was his first stop. There, he'd hand over the gems and get his paycheck. Then, I think he'd hop to his chosen island and set up business."

"If the cops are right, I'm not sure you getting in the middle of any organization big enough to pull off a multi-million dollar heist is such a good idea. Why don't you simply give the investigators a list of questions along with a general idea of outcome and they'll take it from there? Delegation is the cornerstone of a successful business."

"If you it makes you feel better, I'll contact the authorities one more time and tell them my suspicions. I know they have an organized crime unit looking into things, but I don't hold out much hope they'll listen. They seem pretty locked into the TSB's scenario. And delegation isn't appropriate, Dad. Emily isn't business. This is all about me helping solve her problem."

"A knight in shining armor deal."

"Sounds stupid when you put it like that."

"Sounds romantic," said Peter.

"And you would know what about that?"

"Hey, watch the sarcasm, we just got our father/son dialog back on track. Let's just say I was your age once."

"So you'll *recommend* to the investigators that I tag along?"

"Yes, Sir Galahad. It's clear nothing I say will dissuade you. Make your theory call first, and if nothing changes, call Jay Libby directly. I'll ask him to give you any help you require."

Chapter Twenty-Five

Within weeks of the Transcontinental robbery, the warehouse was back to normal, though the authorities had made little headway in locating and arresting Judith Cameron and T.W. Ford. The National Transportation Safety Board theorized the pilot had turned off his transponder after squawking a 'mayday' over New Jersey's Teterboro beacon, dropped below radar, and headed out to sea. Then with the limited amount of fuel usual for the V-Tail Bonanza, the pilot had doubled back to mainland America, setting down somewhere around Miami. There, Captain Ford handed over the diamonds to the criminal organization that hired him.

Jack had no luck presenting his theory to the authorities, so he decided to forge ahead with his team of private investigators from Maine. And as they worked together, Jack garnered more information than he imagined, from the close-knit community of aviators at the Sanford airstrip.

It quickly became clear that T.W. Ford talked often of running an island hopping charter based in Great Abaco, The Bahamas. However, while aviators confirmed what Jack knew—that even with extra fuel tanks, the Bonanza couldn't make it directly there—he was surprised to learn a flight to Bermuda was also impossible. It was only after one of the pilots casually suggested that Ford would have to ditch in the ocean and get picked up, that large pieces of the robbery puzzle fell into place. And when an in-depth look at Ford's military history showed he'd been a Marine parachutist, a wider circle of questioning was undertaken.

It took a week to undercover that a Portland swimming pool had rented time to a man who practiced jumping from the high board fully clothed. The management, who recognized Ford's picture, understood he was rehearsing a stunt for a movie.

Jack was busting to contact Emily and tell her all he'd uncovered. But he didn't want to reveal his findings before he had a definitive answer to the question: "where did Ford and Cameron go?" Therefore, he decamped with his investigators to Bermuda.

Within hours of their arrival, the team was at the marina, under the guise of renting a sport-fishing vessel. And there, a number of local fishermen remembered seeing a commuter-sized airplane disappear after flying low over the ocean. Jack subsequently discovered the event was reported to the Bermudan authorities. However, as no one had come forward to request a search for a missing airplane or persons, the file was relegated to 'pending'.

Jack immediately requested the Bermudan authorities re-open that line of investigation, and armed with the appropriate documentation, he presented himself to his father's insurance company. He hoped his evidence would be enough to prompt them to launch a search. It was not. And after several days of increasingly hostile wrangling, Jack made the decision to go with his gut. With the resources to mount a private recovery, a search area was set.

• • •

It took Jack's team several days to pinpoint the Bonanza in the deep waters of the North American Basin. And when divers were dispatched to search the wreckage, they found what was left of Jude Cameron in the aircraft's cabin. Under the seats, divers also discovered a small quantity of diamonds, and a box cutter. Upon testing the blade, forensic scientists found traces of fabric consistent with that used in a flight suit. And their report suggested that the pilot had killed Cameron, before bailing from the aircraft with the bulk of the diamonds. They also hypothesized that a fishing vessel picked him up and transported him elsewhere.

With murder added to T.W. Ford's warrant list, the investigation was redirected and stepped up. And it wasn't long before the whereabouts of the diamonds was discovered.

• • •

HAMILTON HERALD-BERMUDA

A sport fishing record was broken today when John Peterson and Howard Crane of Boston, Massachusetts, reeled in a short fin Mako shark having a length of fourteen feet and seven inches. The two men decided to mount the trophy and donate it to Kelly's bar, which they frequent on their semi-annual trips to Bermuda. That was when Stanley Ainsworth, taxidermist, discovered the sharks belly held a cache of tin boxes containing thousands of diamonds. Local police and U.S. investigators have been searching for the boxes, and the person who stole them. Sources confirmed today that the boxes, containing diamonds worth twenty million U.S. dollars, were stolen from a Transcontinental Airlines warehouse, in late September. Insurance investigators confirmed that the two anglers will share a ten-percent finder's fee. The whereabouts of the suspected thief, Captain T.W. Ford, as well as the contents of two empty gem boxes found in a downed airplane, recently discovered off our coast, are still a mystery.

• • •

GREAT ABACO STAR-THE BAHAMAS

The island was abuzz today after two local boys made a gruesome discovery, and found a fortune in diamonds on the beach. Law enforcement recovered a partially decomposed torso, with shoulder and arm attached, from a Little Vega tidal pool. A watch, still ticking on the wrist, confirmed the remains were that of T.W. Ford, a courier pilot of Sanford, Maine, U.S.A. Investigators told this reporter, Captain Ford had stolen twenty-six million dollars in diamonds from a Transcontinental Airlines warehouse in September last year. He escaped in his airplane, which ditched some weeks ago, off Bermuda. A police spokesman also told this reporter the airplane held the body of Ford's accomplice, one Judith Cameron of Kew Gardens, New York, U.S.A. It is alleged Ford murdered Cameron, before bailing out of the airplane. The authorities speculate that while being picked up by associates, Ford was attacked and partially eaten by a record-breaking Mako shark recently caught off the Bermuda coast. The partial torso, probably all that was left of the pilot's body, was washed by the current to Great Abaco's shore.

Ocean experts I spoke with confirmed it would not be unusual for the North Atlantic and Antilles currents to have washed up flotsam on Little Vega beach, many miles from where the shark made its initial attack. Insurance appraisers from the United States estimated the value of the diamonds, safely stashed in the zippered arm pockets of the pilot's flight suit, to be around four million U.S. dollars. Clarence Williams, eleven years old, and Jayman Laforce, thirteen, found the diamonds while combing the beach for interesting shells, to sell to tourists. They will share a finder's fee of four hundred thousand U.S. dollars. And while the boys' parents set up an educational trust for the lucky pair, the boys' immediate wish is to buy a boat, so they can go fishing.

Chapter Twenty-Six

Jack could hardly believe that his persistence had paid off. However, when he tried to call Emily and tell her of his progress, she wouldn't take his call. It was only after he spoke to her Attorney Susan Parks that he was connected.

"Emily," he said nervously. "I'm sorry I don't mean to intrude, but I've worked so hard to unravel this mystery, I had to tell you."

"Jack, really, I can only say thank you for everything you've done, but it doesn't change anything between us. I'm not sure I can be what you want me to be. Losing Bill was devastating, and frankly seeing you would only remind me how selfish I was in seeing you in the first place."

"Why? You did nothing untoward. I was the one who made a pass at you. You rejected me at every turn. You have no cause to think you betrayed Bill."

"You don't know what was going on in my head."

"And what was going on?" asked Jack.

"It doesn't matter. Suffice to say, I'm ashamed that for one second I might have given Bill cause to doubt how I felt about him."

"You didn't in my book. Nevertheless, you must have felt something for me to be harboring this level of guilt. Tell me I'm wrong, Emily, and I'll leave you alone and never contact you again."

"You could do that, after having had such intense feelings for me?"

"When I know I can't win, I don't keep playing."

"Spoken like a true gentleman."

"You've said that to me before," Jack replied.

"It seems to fit. So as a gentleman, what if I simply ask you not to contact me again?"

"Won't wash. You have to tell me to my face that you have absolutely no feelings for me at all."

"We're on the phone, Jack."

"Don't split hairs, say it."

"I'd rather go the gentleman route," said Emily.

"See, you can't even say it aloud. I think I have my answer."

"Jack, stop this, it's not healthy."

"Emily, please…I know how much you loved Bill. I know how much you cared and what you were prepared to sacrifice for him. But you're still young; he wouldn't want you to shut yourself off. He'd want you to live, have all those kids you've dreamed of. And damn it, I know he'd want you to give all the love you've bottled up inside to someone else who is devoted to you."

"You didn't even know him. How could you possibly know what he'd want?"

"Because I'm also a man in love with you and I know if anything happened to me that's what I'd want."

Emily couldn't help thinking of the words in Bill's letter, but she wasn't ready to offer her heart to anybody else. "Jack, I'm sorry, I can't talk any longer. I have to go."

"Then I'll call you some other time."

"That would not be the gentlemanly thing to do."

"Where you are concerned, I'm not playing that game," answered Jack. "Tell me you don't care or face the consequences."

"And what might they be?"

"Eternal devotion from an honest, hardworking man who adores you."

"Excuse me?"

"Do I have to spell it out? I love you, now and forever."

"And a year," whispered Emily.

"Sorry, what did you say?" asked Jack.

As Bill's words echoed, timeless and joyful in Emily's head, she said goodbye and set down the phone.

Chapter Twenty-Seven

Press cameras exploded as Joe opened the door to the limousine. The diminutive Susan Parks emerged to face the impressive façade of the courthouse, and questions began firing at her from all sides. She ignored the barrage, and calmly straightened her skirt and jacket. And as she reached for her briefcase, her phone rang.

"Yes, I understand, thank you." Susan ducked back into the limo. "Don't look so worried, Emily. That was my office. The bulk of the Walvis Bay diamonds have been recovered and they've had confirmation that both Jude Cameron and T.W. Ford are dead. Also, your colleagues from Transcontinental are all in court. It seems you weren't the only one holding back on suspecting Jude of warehouse robberies. There's a bunch of agents with statements that will bolster your cause."

Emily smiled thinly. "All this because of Jack's interventions?"

"For the most part, I'd say yes. Jack not only went out on a limb with his hunch about Bermuda. But he and his father purchased a huge interest in Transcontinental, and have been relentless in wheedling out the inadequacies at the warehouse. Their involvement goes way beyond any feelings they might have towards you. They've been all about fixing a significant and ongoing problem, and making things right. Jack's been calling me every day for weeks; he's really come through for you."

Emily blushed. "I realize that."

"So will you speak to him now?"

"I'm not sure I'm ready."

"You know he's here and he's going to want to speak to you, so ready or not, put your game face on. But first we have some obstruction of justice issues to deal with."

"Okay," said Emily nervously. "Let's do this."

As Emily stepped from the car, it was clear who the paparazzi had come to see. Flashbulbs exploded as she stepped forward, and when the jostling gaggle of reporters closed in, Emily felt Susan's hand about her elbow.

"It's less than fifty yards to the courthouse doors. Look straight ahead and whatever happens, keep walking."

Emily walked confidently, wondering what sort of spin the vultures of the press would put on her calm appearance. She knew it was impossible to escape criticism, for it had been with her for some time.

In fact, since Bill's death, so-called society mavens—never friends of her straight-talking style—had hounded her with phone calls and e-mails. She'd spoken to no one, but that didn't stop their presses buzzing with a condescending stream of misinformation about the scheming cargo agent who'd made good. Reading it their way, Emily was a gold digger who stumbled upon a dying man twice her age, and manipulated him into leaving her millions in cash, real estate, and business interests. And while it bothered her at first, she quickly accepted that true friends were aware she'd never asked Bill for anything. There was no doubt however that even a shallow dig into Emily's past, would reveal that before and during her time with Bill, she'd made certain dubious life choices. Now, it was time to pay for those choices, and she was ready for whatever the court dictated.

. . .

The courthouse hushed as the bailiff asked everyone to stand.

Anyone seeing the women for the first time would be struck by their dissimilarities. Emily Wilks, tall and elegant, impeccably dressed in one of the expensive designer suits Bill had purchased for her. Susan Parks, short and matronly, conservative of dress reeking of establishment mores. But the diminutive attorney with the dowdy personality held her own in or out, of a courtroom, and was known for her blistering rebuttals. Those who might dismiss her based on appearance alone were left smarting from the barbs of her meticulous research, prodigious memory, and knowledge of the law. And while her measured disregard for urgency often caused impatience and irritation in her peers, she invariably highlighted that as a character flaw in her opponent. Susan's prime directive was to inspire confidence in her client, and if she had to step on toes and bruise egos to accomplish that, she would.

When Judge Davis Williams took his seat to preside over the hearing, Susan's smile was imperceptible. She felt Emily fearfully stiffening next to her, and touched her arm in a gesture of friendship and understanding. Susan might be the consummate professional, but she had a flair for the dramatic.

And it was no coincidence Judge Williams was presiding over this case. He came from a wealthy family of old money, had married a waitress twenty-five years his junior, and of one thing at the very least, attorney Susan Parks could be sure. This judge would understand an older man's love for a much younger woman.

• • •

When Judge Williams' gavel came down, Susan's defense had been on-point and compelling. Nevertheless, Emily was ordered to report to Beacon minimum-security prison the following day. Her five-month sentence would be followed by a two-year probationary period, during which time she would not be allowed to leave the United States.

. . .

As Susan and Emily descended the courthouse steps, the disappointed press, who'd been hoping for some sort of rich-bitch blame-anyone-but-me scenario, had dispersed. Joe was waiting with the limo door open chatting to a familiar blond.

"I see Jack is with Joe," said Susan. "I have some calls to make so why don't you go visit a while. Hey, Joe, would you step this way a minute? I have some questions for you."

Coming alongside the vehicle, Emily extended her hand to Jack. "Thank you for everything you did in there."

He brushed his lips against her knuckles, and brought her hand to rest on his heart. "I said I'd find a way to help you."

Emily smiled. "Buying a chunk of an airline was a bit extreme."

"Worked, didn't it? Besides, Dad bought it, not me."

"Dad? So it appears you two are speaking."

Jack smiled. "Thanks to you."

"Me? I don't even know him."

"You brought us together. After Monaco, he could see I was finally passionate about something and it blossomed from there."

"I'm glad for you both, Jack; family is important. What will you do now?"

"What do you mean?"

"Susan told me you turned down the big job in the city. So, will you go back to South Africa, or continue giving yacht tours?"

"I'll be here with you."

"Don't be silly," said Emily. "I'll be in prison."

"Not for long."

"Five months." Emily fought to keep her emotions under control, and attempted to remove her hand. Jack held it fast, an unconditional devotion she so well remembered in his eyes.

"Emily, please don't send me away," he whispered. "I can't just *stop* loving you."

"Love? Jack, please, be sensible. What we had in Monaco wasn't love, it was a flirtation. We were two ships passing in the night."

"Now who's getting quotes off a crackerjack box? I don't believe you. You're not that good an actress."

"Okay. So I admit it. The few hours we had *were* special. But love is much deeper. Love is what I felt for Bill. Love is being willing to live or die for someone, to set your life aside and do anything, go anywhere, to make that person feel better."

"Didn't I just do that?"

Emily blushed. "I suppose you did, but it doesn't change anything between us."

"You can stand there, look me in the eyes and honestly tell me there is no chance that one day you might feel the same about me as you did about Bill?"

"Er…I don't know. There's too much going on. I have obligations to meet before I can even think about a relationship. This just isn't the time for us."

"I can't bear to think about you alone in prison, and I want you to know, I'll be here. Do whatever needs to be done, be whoever you want me to be, as long as you'll consider the possibility. Are 'we' possible, or am I crazy? Did I so completely misunderstand what we had in Monaco?"

Emily looked at him with tears welling, pulled her hand from his, and got into the limousine.

Jack bent down and saw she was quietly sobbing. "We belong together Emily, our being together is cosmic; you said that. Please don't push me away."

"Jack, I'm sorry. I don't know how else to feel right now."

Before Jack could say anything further, Susan returned. "Give her some time Jack," she whispered. "She's not going anywhere for a few months." Then she slid in beside Emily and closed the door.

As the car pulled away, Jack never imagined he could feel so desolate. Emily was being taken from him again. Then it began to rain. With knuckles tight against his lips, he could no longer fight back tears. His soul emptied, trickling to who knows where like the rain in the gutter at his feet. His sorrow was abject, and it was fitting the heavens were shedding the same miserable tears as he. And as the limousine drifted on, ten, twenty, thirty yards— it might as well have been light years. Then it stopped. He was paralyzed as it reversed, and pulled alongside him.

When the rear window slid down, Emily was leaning across Susan. "Get in your car before you catch pneumonia. You know where I'll be after tomorrow; come visit me."

It was raining steadily as the limousine sped away, and Jack cried. But this time they were happy tears. Then he smiled. Walking to his car, he smiled. Dripping water all over his expensive upholstery, he smiled. Brushing aside sodden hair as he spotted his reflection in the rear-view mirror, he smiled. This was the most wonderful day of his life, and he couldn't stop smiling.

Chapter Twenty-Eight

Jack rented a house outside the prison and visited Emily every day during her incarceration. Early on, she used her visiting hours for the lawyers and accountants who were keeping her abreast of the empire left to her by Bill. However, she didn't want to lose Jack's company, and asked him to sit in on the meetings.

Each day after she completed the tasks assigned to her by the prison authority, Jack arrived with the Bailey Corporation advisors. They educated the pair on every facet of Emily's companies, and during those sessions, it became clear how astute and knowledgeable Jack was about international finance, and global commerce. His formal education allowed him to quickly navigate the maze of the Bailey empire, and whenever Emily had a question or needed an opinion, he had the answer. Moreover, his patience with her lack of knowledge was boundless, and he proved not only to be an invaluable friend, but an excellent teacher. He simply explained business issues, helped her make commercial decisions, and she readily allowed him to get involved in executive decision-making.

By the time Emily had completed four of her five-month sentence; it was obvious to those around them, that she and Jack were each half of what was a very powerful whole. So it was natural that when an opportunity presented itself, Jack was appointed to the position of Director of International Finance and Development. He blossomed, assuming a level of expertise even seasoned veterans of Bailey Corporation admired.

And with his prodigious intellect, and sensitive business savvy, his quiet confidence began to win over Emily.

Chapter Twenty-Nine

Jack was nervous as he paced back and forth in front of the limousine. And looking at his watch, he counted down the seconds to Emily's release. During the entire time of her incarceration, there had been no mention of Monaco, and their flirtation had become but a special memory. And though Jack had proved his devotion in a business sense, he still wasn't sure whether his accomplishments were enough to convince Emily of the depth of his feelings for her. Now, seeing her in the distance, his emotions welled, and he had no doubt on some level, they would spend the rest of their lives together.

As Emily approached Beacon's checkpoint, Joe was out of the limo and walking to meet her. She could see Jack pacing nervously beside the vehicle, and couldn't help giggling at the absurdity of it all. He'd leaped outside his privileged box and chased her half way around the world, just to make sure she was all right. He'd given up a large part of his inheritance and several months of life, to play a part in hers. And he'd successfully taken on a major role in the Bailey empire, so that her promise to Bill remained a reality.

Now, the high powered executive, with the wealth and power to move mountains, paced back and forth like a prom date, building courage to knock on the door of her father's house.

After shaking hands with the guards, Emily stepped through the release gate. "Hi, brother," she said, hugging Joe like she'd been gone for twenty years. "Fresh air at last and it is so good to be free."

"Know what you mean, and for an ex con, you smell damn good."

She cuffed him. "Watch it, fly boy, I'm still the one paying your salary."

Joe saluted smartly. "Yes, ma'am." He picked up Emily's bag and dropped an arm over her shoulder. "So where would you kids like to go?"

Emily smiled. "Judging by Jack's pacing, he either wants to pee very badly, or go home and talk."

"You up for that?"

"The peeing or the talking?"

"Yikes, you sure have loosened up a notch since being inside."

She laughed aloud. "Let's go home, wisenheimer."

As Joe put Emily's bag in the trunk, she looked back at the prison. If nothing else, her confinement had given her an opportunity to see what was important, who she could trust, and how she wanted to conduct the rest of her life. And now standing beside Jack, she felt no distance between them. "How long have you been pacing about out here?"

"On and off, five months."

"And what did all this pacing accomplish?"

"Lost a little weight, wore out two pairs of my good shoes, and realized that if I have to do it again, I'm taking a hostage."

"That's pretty heavy for my first minutes of freedom."

"Gets worse."

"How so?"

Jack took Emily's hand. "I have absolutely no doubt I love you more than life itself."

"Now that's a statement."

"It can't be any surprise."

"It's not. But at the very least, I expected a bunch of flowers with the lovey-dovey stuff."

Jack leaned inside the limo, and pulled out a bouquet. "Iris and sunflowers…your favorites, right?"

"Why, thank you, kind sir, indeed they are."

"So do I get a thank-you kiss?"

Emily smiled. "You're impossible. Get in the car; we have a lot to talk about."

Chapter Thirty

Several months had passed since Emily's incarceration and along with becoming an indispensable part of the Bailey Corporation, Jack now lived at Harrington Hall. He lived in the west wing, while Emily lived in the east, but she had never permitted him to rekindle their flirtation in Monaco. It was at times, difficult for him, but Jack knew why things had to change between them. Nevertheless, he diligently proved his business worth, improving the fortunes of Bailey Corp, and willingly fulfilled the company's social duties as if he were Emily's husband. It wasn't ideal, but as long as he could be with her every day, talk to her, and drink in her beauty, wit and intelligence, he was content.

● ● ●

Sun poured through the window of Jack's sitting room as he sipped coffee. Being Saturday, he and Emily generally took out the horses and circulated the estate checking for nonexistent fence problems.

He was about to pull on his boots and go down to breakfast, when there was a tap on his door. Servants knocked and came directly in, so when the door remained closed he opened it. It was Emily, and she was carrying a breakfast tray.

"Hello," said Jack. "I didn't order breakfast in bed."

"I did, and it bothered me that you might be alone in that huge dining room. So I changed my mind and thought we might share this."

"Are you always so purposeful when something bothers you?"

"Bother me and you'll find out."

Jack could see she wasn't wearing the wedding ring Bill had given her. "I want to bother you, but in a non-breakfast way."

"Well let's discuss that, because frankly, I'm over breakfast."

"Is that rhetorical?" asked Jack. "Or do you mean what I think you mean?"

Emily smiled. "I'm not sure I know if I mean what you think I mean."

"Well that makes it crystal clear. I am officially lost. Who is doing what for whom?"

"I'm sure there have been a million occasions, but lately I've noticed that something about you is most definitely bothering me."

Jack ran a hand down her arm. "In a good way?"

Emily smiled. "Oh yes, in a very good way."

As Emily squeezed by Jack, she could sense the tension between them. It was the good kind. "Just let me set this down, I want to check something." She reached to unbuckle his belt, and his breathing quickened. "My, my, Mr. Clemmons," she whispered. "It does seem my checking on you in somewhat discombobulating."

Jack grinned. "It is, but in the good way previously mentioned."

"Is your discombobulation such that you need to lie down?"

"That might be advisable," he said, trying not to laugh.

"I believe there is an appropriate lounging spot in the other room."

Jack took her hand and brought it to his lips. "Emily, is this really happening or am I having another of those highly inappropriate dreams?"

"I have no idea," she giggled. "What usually happens next?" She put a hand down the front of his pants.

Jack smiled. "Yeah, that's about it. That's what usually happens next."

"And how about this?" she asked as she kissed him passionately.

"Yup," said Jack breathlessly. "It's that dream again."

"Umm," said Emily, backing away. "Then I think I may have to take the bull by the horns and jump outside my comfortable little box."

"I seem to remember, a lifetime ago, you told me to do that."

"I most certainly did and look what a superb job you made of it. So what happens next? Hypothetically…in this dream?"

Jack walked into the bedroom, stripped off, and dove onto the bed. "You coming in?" he asked. "Or should I start without you?"

Emily laughed aloud. "Oh come on. Clothes all over the floor, straight down to business; surely you can do better than that?"

"No," said Jack matter-of-factly. "This is my dream. You walk in, I strip, we make love. Ten minutes tops. Then I wake, climb into a cold shower and start work."

"That is so sad." Emily pulled off her sweater, and stepped out of her pants. "But it's your dream." She was acutely aware of the effect her delaying tactics were having.

"Are you going to stop fooling around, and join me?"

"What's the hurry, Mr. Clemmons; do you have somewhere else to go?" Emily noted the pale slashes interrupting his all-over tan. "Are those from the accident?"

"Yup." Jack patted the bed next to him. "Time's a'wasting."

Emily sashayed to the bed, but when he reached for her, she backed away. "Now it's my dream…no touching." She placed the tip of her index finger in her mouth, and traced each of his scars with her moist fingertip.

Electrifying pulses surged through Jack's body. "That's not fair," he whispered, attempting to pull her atop him.

She stepped back and peeled off her bra and panties. "Whoever said love was fair."

Jack pushed onto his elbow to watch her. "So are you saying this is love?"

"I'm not sure." Emily climbed on the bed, and straddled his lap. "Umm, that feels good, and it seems certain parts of you might be bordering on sure."

Moving to a tune in her head Emily rocked back and forth. However, as soon as she felt Jack's crescendo build, she abruptly moved away from his passion-fired body. "I have an experiment," she said breathlessly.

"Na-ah, come back, that's not in my dream."

Emily smiled. "It is in mine, and I need to get something."

"I need you here, in this bed, right now." Jack lunged at her.

"No sir. I get the distinct feeling a certain area of your education is sadly lacking. I want to get you up to speed."

"God, you're serious."

"I most definitely am." Emily snickered. "Excuse the expression, but are you up for it?"

Jack looked down. "Well right now, I'd have to say that's a maybe. But God help me, what do you have in mind?"

"Stay there, lie still and close your eyes." Emily went to her breakfast tray and uncovered clotted cream next to the strawberries.

"What's happening?" asked a mildly concerned Jack.

"I'm about to have my favorite breakfast." Emily opened the jar of cream and dropped a large dollop on his diminishing erection.

"Yikes, that's bloody cold," he said, eyes suddenly open.

"Trust me, eyes shut," she whispered. At first lapping and nipping, she quickly resurrected his passion. Then she took him full in her mouth, and drew his length slowly back and forth. When his low moan let her know he had fully warmed to her ministrations, Emily backed off again, and stood beside the bed. "Come on, I have goodies for the shower." She attempted to pull him to his feet.

Jack held tight to her hand. "Not this time, missy, I have waited far too long. No more games." He pulled her onto the bed, and flipping her on her back, entered her.

Within minutes, the synchronous rhythm of their bodies produced an explosive satisfaction neither had known before.

...

Somewhere between the ecstasy that was Emily, and the misery that would be his life without her, Jack drifted into dreams. There was no doubt she did amazing things to his body. But more than that, when he looked deep into his mind's eye, he saw them together, with children, dogs, and abundant laughter in a huge house. And it was Harrington Hall. It was a life he'd always wanted. A life where comfort and love enveloped him, rolling hills surrounded him, and his tiny corner of the universe was blissfully content.

And as he drifted back to sleep and came upon his hometown of Walvis Bay, he saw himself younger, reading everything he could find on the subject of love. It reminded him that like many children without a nurturing childhood, he never really knew what 'love' was.

Now, with some wisdom gleaned from the intervening years, and clinical over-analysis behind him, Jack knew Emily was as near as he'd ever get to his ideal. And the dream both comforted and bothered him. For as he drifted from memory to memory, seeing women he bedded, those who had done little more than lie back and make him sweat, Emily stood out, different in every way. Not only was she bright, funny and intelligent, but she was totally sure about everything she did. She didn't seem to care what people thought of her, and just being with her gave him strength. She challenged his mind, and fed his body what it wanted. She made him beg for more—and for mercy—at the same time. But most important, she recognized his fears and liberated his soul.

...

Jack woke with a start, his mind unquestionably set, and as he kissed Emily's shoulder, she moaned softly. Draping his arm about her, he buried his face between her shoulders, breathing in the fragrance of her skin. Then shifting his body, he eased her towards him. When her eyes opened, he basked in the intense green that had haunted his soul.

"Emily," he whispered. "Will you marry me?"

"Because of one roll in the hay?"

"Darling, be serious. This is not a knee-jerk impulse. I've dreamed about this moment from the beginning."

She pecked him on the nose. "Then don't spoil it."

"Don't you want to marry me?"

"I haven't made up my mind yet."

Jack frowned. "I asked you once if you could ever love me like you loved Bill."

"And I answered, 'I don't know, this isn't the time for us'."

"Doesn't this qualify?"

Emily smiled and slipped from the bed. "Be patient, darling. When I'm sure, you'll be the first to know."

• • •

Jack watched her beautifully proportioned body disappear into the bathroom, and then closed his eyes. *How could his perfect woman finally be in his bed? And would she ever want him as much as he wanted her?* He'd lain back and hardly moved as Emily made love to him, but he was exhausted. And as he tuned his senses, listening to the water and Emily humming a tune he didn't recognize, he felt invincible.

Breathing deep to counter the exquisite remembrance, Jack realized Emily's lovemaking was so much more than the clinical act he'd previously experienced. She might exhaust him, and force every emotion to the surface, but she gave him peace, and soothed his soul. He didn't know how or why, but his feelings for her came from so deep inside, from so primeval a place they defied understanding. But he knew for certain her unconditional passion gave him sublime contentment, and he never wanted to be without it again.

He rose from bed with a smile on his face, and joined Emily in the shower.

Chapter Thirty-One

It was early October, two years after Bill's death, and Jack was reviewing a proposal to open a new diamond-cutting house in Antwerp. It would receive gems from the mines of Walvis Bay Holdings, and as he waded through the stack of agreements, Jack could see how Peter Clemmons had become so successful. Every "i" was dotted and "t" crossed. The agreements were flawless and fair, and he couldn't see why anyone would not want to do business with his father. As he added the contracts to a pile of items for Emily's review, there was a knock at the door.

Brothers came in with a bottle of champagne, placed it on the credenza and quietly departed.

Jack was about to say he'd not ordered wine, when he spotted Emily in the doorway. "Hello," he grinned. "What's going on? I know it's not my birthday, or yours, and I haven't shown you the latest acquisition; so why are we celebrating?"

"It's time," Emily said, moving slowly toward him.

"And you are in a peignoir because?"

There was no doubt Emily was naked beneath the robe. "I thought you might like an early lunch."

Jack grinned. "Lunch? Are you hiding canapés under that thing?"

She stopped beside Jack's chair. "I thought about it, and spoke to Mrs. Hudson about those shrimp things you love. Then decided on something all my own."

"Something all your own, eh? With no care that turning up in a nightie might totally traumatize old Brothers?"

"That's impossible," she replied. "Whatever we get up to, he'll soldier along as if nothing is happening."

Jack grinned. "And what exactly is happening?"

"May I sit?"

"You're the boss. Feel free."

Emily positioned herself astride him.

Jack brushed a lock of hair from her face. "Now I know why all the chairs are without arms."

"Would you prefer a chair with arms, I can have one broug—"

"No, I'm good. This is, er, nice, er, comfortable."

"It is, isn't it? But it seems you're breathing is somewhat labored, Mr. Clemmons. Are you in distress again? It seems to be a frequent occurrence during our personal time together."

Jack grinned. "And you're surprised when you come to me half naked in the middle of the day?"

"Seems that as the boss, I may choose the dress code, and assign whatever meeting time I feel appropriate to ensure an uptick in staff morale."

Jack laughed aloud. "Uptick in staff morale. Now that's funny."

"So, in keeping with my position, is there something I can get you? Glass of water? A little oxygen?"

"I've been told should I collapse from, shall we say, acute anxiety, that mouth-to-mouth resuscitation is generally administered."

"I can call Joe," said Emily coyly. "He's not only a pilot, but a fully accredited EMT."

"Let's not bother him right now," smirked Jack. "Besides, that peignoir is pretty revealing. Brothers might be used to it, but I'm not sure Joe's role of part-time medicine man allows him access to a half-naked boss."

"What about your wife?"

"Excuse me?"

"Will you marry me, Jack Clemmons?" Emily smiled, and locked her mouth on his.

Chapter Thirty-Two

Nobody could have imagined just how much noise two very small babies could make. Sophie and Bailey Clemmons made no bones about the fact they were here and shocked by the whole affair. But as the nurses at Saratoga Samaritan placed the second twin in Jack's arms, the noise quieted.

"So, darling," said Jack. "I think these two are taking after you. Perfectly content as long as I hold them."

"And don't you forget it."

"So, do you still want to go directly to Lake Point?"

Emily nodded. "A promise is a promise."

• • •

Emily held tightly onto the twins as Jack drove the golf cart to Lake Point. She couldn't help looking at him and could hardly believe that her feelings for him outstripped those she had for Bill. She knew from the beginning that he was a younger version of her first love, but she could never have imagined how effortless it was to have him in her life. She had wanted time to make sure her feelings for him were not some sort of backlash, some yearning to recapture a flirtatious moment in time. Now, with marriage and babies, she realized how perfectly their time together passed. He lit up their space and made her whole, and now they had two smaller versions of themselves, she loved him so desperately it hurt. Emily would never forget how comfortable it was to be with Bill, but with Jack, that comfort was compounded by their mutual goal to raise a large family.

It also helped that whatever they did together, however much they were on, or off, track about something, they ended up laughing. And she felt so in harmony with him, she couldn't imagine life without him. She had thought Bill was everything to her, but she now realized her complete and true love was Jack. He was that 'one' she would live or die for, and without question, do anything, go anywhere, to make him feel better.

• • •

Jack parked opposite the spot where Emily had scattered Bill's ashes, and helped her to the water's edge. Then, as he opened a bottle of champagne to toast Bill's memory, he watched her slowly pan the babies from left to right. They were uncharacteristically quiet in the warm air amid Harrington's rolling hills and as Jack's eyes remained on his wife, she had a look of absolute serenity he'd not seen before.

Then he heard her whisper.

"Say hello to Uncle Bill, my beautiful babies. He always got what he wanted and he knew that, given time, love will find a way."

More From This Author
(From *Desperate Obsession*)

Jake and a spare chair were under siege at his usual table in the airport coffee shop, and when he saw Alex, striking in her Europa Airways uniform, a head taller than the average woman, he waved. She meandered toward him, and when her leg straddled the pile of baggage surrounding his table, he gave up defense of the chair. "Sit," he ordered, pecking her on both cheeks, "the vultures are circling."

"Nice work, Detective, you demonstrate a real flair for crowd control."

"Not funny, Miss I'll-be-there-at-three-forty-five. What kept you?"

"You can't have been here long."

"Twenty fun-filled minutes, in which time I barely avoided an all-out brawl with the Austrian Sumo wrestler over there." His head inclined toward a large lady in loden green, wearing a Tyrolean hat with a feather.

"Sorry, sweetie," said Alex. "The traffic was horrendous. Then I got to the parking lot and couldn't find my key card."

"I'll never understand how someone so outwardly put together can be so hopelessly absentminded."

"All part of my charm. Now shush, there's more. Terri what's-her-name from Gulf Air—big boobs, Vampira fingernails?"

"Blond with orange streaks?"

"Highlights, you plebe. So you do know her?"

"I know of her."

"She stopped me and asked about you."

"Me?"

"Yes 'me,' you sneaky dog. What've you been up to?"

"Not her, that's for sure, she's a man-eater. You know she and Eddie Barstow were playing more than footsie in a storage locker at the last customs party. Suffice to say he wore turtlenecks for a week, and God knows what his back looked like after tangling with those nails."

"Well, Eddie Barstow couldn't have made much of an impression, because her entire conversation was about you."

"Why the hell would she ask about me? We barely know each other. However, I do know she has a thing for cops…do you?"

"Do I what?"

"Have a thing for cops?"

"Oh, I get it, a fishing expedition." Alex patted Jake's hand. "Just one ruggedly handsome boy next door type."

"I'm ruggedly handsome?"

Alex smiled. "Don't get too confident, I still haven't found out if you have any money."

"Typical female." He felt the saucer atop her coffee cup and removed it. "Here, it's still warm."

"Ugh, what is that?"

"Cappuccino the way you like it."

"I like a sprinkle of chocolate, not a crust."

"Pretty vile, huh?" Jake wagged his finger. "You should've been here on time."

Alex's eyes narrowed in her come-hell-or-high-water look as she brought the cup to her mouth.

"Nah-ah, don't do it, Alex." Jake reached for the cup. "Seriously, you do not have to drink that. I just wanted to see if you would."

She chugged the brew and replaced cup against saucer with a triumphant chink. "Impressive, no?"

"See, that's exactly what I mean. I say don't do it, you do; you are without doubt the most contrary female I've ever known. And don't give me 'the face.' A spanking is what you need—a good old-fashioned, over-the-knee thrashing."

"You and whose army, Mr. Big Time Special Branch Detective Inspector?"

"Like you don't think I'll do it. Jeez, if we weren't on duty.. "

"Yeah, duty, it's a bitch. We spend our life doing our duty."

"Well, I was joking," Jake said, "but even for you, that's cynical. What's up?"

"Nothing, just one of those days."

"No, it's not. I'm your best friend, I know you. We've been doing this coffee klatch thing since our stint at the grief support group and I've never seen you like this." As darkness clouded Alex's eyes, Jake's memory kicked in. Pushing the date button on his watch, September 10 flashed. "Damn it all, Alex, why are you here? Take a couple of days off—nobody will think badly of you."

"The tenth was the last time I spoke to him before the towers came down and he was just *gone*. I wouldn't do it then and I can't do it now. Remember the first time we met; I was so distracted I dinged your car?"

"Of course I do, it brought us together. Uh-oh, don't tell me you hit me in the parking lot."

"Not today, but I was thinking about some things on the way in, the traffic, the crowds, and people rushing all over the world getting nowhere fast." Her eyes glazed over. "Travel used to be enjoyable—you turned up, you flew off. It was fun."

"A lot's happened to change that."

"Amen to that. At least you've been my rock."

"That's me, solid, dependable…gray." He flipped the lapels of his suit jacket.

She smiled. "I do prefer you in navy."

"That's tomorrow. You really okay?"

"I am, promise. It's the whole uniform, toe the line, and fly the flag thing. It gets me every time."

"Well, I can't do too much about being a cop for another few years. But your husband left you well provided for; you can quit the airline biz anytime you want. Why don't you get out and see some of the world you're helping everyone else enjoy?"

"Maybe I will. After all, I'm in passenger handling, it's not like I'm indispensable."

"Some of us might challenge that. I'd be pretty bummed if you weren't in my life."

"That's so sweet, now I know why Jessie fell for you." Alex touched Jake's hand. "Why am I being so self-absorbed, you must miss her too?"

"I do, but the last thing she said to me was that she wanted me to move on."

"You can't just forget you had a fiancée."

"It's not about forgetting. It's about finding a new normal. If you don't, the emptiness will drive you mad."

"You're right, as always. And I know in my heart Joe would want the same. Maybe that's why I'm so torn today, I'm a little frightened, but ready to move on."

Jake's heart skipped a beat. This was his opportunity to tell Alex how he truly felt about her. "Do you have anyone in mind?"

She smiled. "I've been thinking that maybe—" A rucksack swiped her from behind. "Yowch!"

"Oops, sorry, ma'am," mumbled a lanky youth through his beard.

Alex scooted her chair closer to the table.

"That's new," said Jake.

"The thinking or the yowch?"

"The 'ma'am.' How's it feel to join the rest of us on the road to decrepitude?"

"I'm thirty-eight, as are you, and I for one am not ready to hang up my dancing shoes." Alex looked around. "But look at this place. It's fast approaching bedlam and survival of the fittest. Tell me one more time why we put ourselves through this every day?"

"We're airport junkies."

"But it's all consuming; we spend our lives here."

"So seriously, quit doing it," Jake said.

"Don't think I can, working fills the void."

"Then at least apply for some vacation time, take a cruise, have an adventure."

"Alone?"

"You won't be alone for long. On second thoughts, I'm not sure the adventure thing would sit entirely well with me."

"Oooh…interesting statement…little green monster raising its ugly head?"

"Are you saying I'm jealous?"

Alex held up thumb and forefinger. "Little bit."

"Or maybe it's because I know you, your track record isn't good. You attract bleeding hearts like lint. Remember that guy who sent you photocopies of his butt because you said he looked good in jeans? Or the idiot who stuck decals all over your brand new car because you admired his psychedelic bus? What might have happened if I hadn't spoken with both of them?"

"I get the picture: me silly girl, you big, strong protector."

"This is serious, Alex; they could have been nut cases."

"I have a bunch of brothers who could redirect any misplaced infatuation."

"Oh yeah, white bread vanilla businessmen one and all."

"Yikes, that's pretty harsh."

"Maybe. I mean, they're nice guys but I'm seeing lovers not fighters. What could they possibly know about the less-than-gentle art of persuasion?"

"Simon's something of a jock, but on the whole, you're probably right," Alex admitted.

"You know darn well I'm right. I'm always bailing you out of some crazy escapade."

"So how about bailing me out of this afternoon's mess? According to the news, fog was so bad this morning there was no movement in or out for over five hours. This evening could be the mother of all log-jams."

"If you hit overload, call me. I'll use my incredible level of police authority to declare an airport emergency, clear the building, and give you a breather."

"Then who clears that backlog, Sherlock?"

"Right, forgot about a future backlog on top of the current backlog. Emergency, bad idea, guess this time you're on your own."

"Typical male."

"Touché. But look, Alex, all kidding aside, I'm also getting pretty fed up fighting through passengers. We've been doing this coffee shop thing forever, pussy footing around the real thing. We should meet somewhere else—outside work. A bar, restaurant maybe. Would you like to—" *Beep, beep, beep.* Jake hit the message button on his pager. "Jeez, they stopped one of my terrorist watch-list guys in arrivals."

"Terrorist?"

"Yeah, and I didn't tell you that. Look, I have to go. How about we meet—" The beeper squawked again. "Damn, this one's big. Sorry, Alex, gotta go, but we have to talk."

Alex checked her watch. "Good grief, is that the time? I have to get going too, call me later?" She kissed her fingertips, pressed them lightly on his forehead, and wound her way back into the terminal.

Jake watched until he could no longer distinguish her uniform, pressed his own fingers on the spot she touched, and brought them down to brush his lips. *Beep, beep, beep.* "Jeez, yeah right, I got it, I'm on the way."

In the mood for more Crimson Romance?
Check out *In the Shadow of Greed*
by Nancy Weeks
at *CrimsonRomance.com*.

About the Author

Born and raised in Warwickshire, England, Anji immigrated to the United States in 1986, and now resides in Northern Arizona. She has written six novels, *The Cormorant Club, Desperate Obsession, Lonely Hearts Cry, How Many Freakin' Frogs Do You Have To Kiss?, Love is in the Air, and Love Will Find A Way.* She is a member of the Mystery Writers of America, Romance Writers of America, NARWA, RWA-Kiss of Death, and the Chick-lit Writers of the World.